"Janelle, I'm sixteen years old and I've never had a date," Carley said. "Why do you suppose that is? Could it be because I'm not pretty? Why isn't my wonderful personality taken into consideration?"

"Now you're being sarcastic."

"No. I'm being realistic. I'm never going to have a date. No guy's ever going to ask me out anywhere in public."

Janelle sighed heavily. "I know it seems that way now."

"You bet it does."

"Kyle might just be the one if you'd give him half a chance."

"So long as he's blind and so long as we don't have to mingle with the rest of the world, Kyle and I can have a thing for each other. But the minute his vision clears, it'll be over between us. Trust me. I know what I'm talking about."

I'll Be
Seeing You

Lurlene McDaniel

I'll Be
Seeing You

BANTAM BOOKS
NEW YORK • TORONTO • LONDON • SYDNEY • AUCKLAND

RL 5.6, ages 012 and up

I'LL BE SEEING YOU

A Bantam Book / July 1996

ISBN 0-553-56718-7

Published simultaneously in the United States and Canada

Bantam Books are published by Bantam Books, a division of
Random House, Inc. Its trademark, consisting of the words "Bantam
Books" and the portrayal of a rooster, is Registered in U.S. Patent
and Trademark Office and in other countries. Marca Registrada.
Bantam Books, 1540 Broadway, New York, New York 10036.

PRINTED IN THE UNITED STATES OF AMERICA

18

For Christy Brown,
a real winner

"He has made everything beautiful in its time."

(Ecclesiastes 3:11)

One

"Give it a rest, Reba!" Carley Mattea said. Only her friend Reba Conroy could get excited about a new patient admitted to their floor. "We're not Knoxville General's social committee," Carley added. She balanced on her crutches, flipped the gears on Reba's electric wheelchair, and guided it backward toward Carley's room. Her new friend was an incredible optimist. Carley couldn't understand it.

"I heard his name's Kyle Westin," Reba reported. "I asked a nurse and she said he's from Oak Ridge, like you. Maybe he even goes to the same high school. Wouldn't that be a fabulous coincidence? You come to the hospital but end up making friends with a cool boy."

"You're all the new friends I want to make while I'm here, Reba." Carley tried to smile sweetly. Reba was too much, talking about boys. A few days before, Carley had undergone surgery on her leg for a nasty break that had occurred the day after Christmas. An infection had landed her in the hospital on IV antibiotics. Carley wasn't so sick that she was confined to bed, but she'd been bored stiff. Then Reba had rolled into her room and started a conversation. Now it seemed as if they'd known each other forever.

"I like making new friends," Reba volunteered. "It's fun."

Carley had a totally different attitude about meeting new people. Actually, the only place she felt comfortable was in the hospital. People were used to kids with problems, so they didn't stare at her as much. Sure, a broken leg was a common enough thing to see, but her face—*that* was a different matter.

Carley propped her crutches against a

chair and struggled up onto her hospital bed, where she punched the TV remote control button. "Oak Ridge High School isn't so small that I wouldn't remember a guy named Kyle Westin, and I've never heard of him. Besides, I'm sure we'd never end up in the same crowd."

"Would you please turn that dumb thing off? We have strategy to discuss."

"Strategy?"

"Sure. Like how we can meet him . . . get to know him."

Carley rolled her eyes. "I don't want to meet him. He probably doesn't want to meet anyone either."

"He's just been admitted. Give him a day or so. He'll loosen up."

"From the back he looks perfectly normal," Carley said, turning up the volume with the remote control. "Believe me, Reba, normal guys aren't interested in girls like me."

The eighth floor of the giant hospital was reserved for adolescent patients with a variety of medical problems. With his face turned to the wall and his covers pulled up to his shoulders, there was no guessing what might be wrong with Kyle Westin.

Reba looked crestfallen, and Carley momentarily regretted dashing the fourteen-year-old girl's good spirits. *It's for her own good,* Carley told herself. Carley had learned early on that if she didn't set her expectations too high, she didn't get hurt. "Look, I didn't mean to rain on your parade. I'm sure Kyle will become one of the 'gang' once he realizes that he's a prisoner and there's nothing he can do about it." She leaned forward conspiratorially. "Unless, of course, he makes a rope out of his bedsheets and lowers himself out the window."

Reba giggled. "You're so funny."

"Sure, a real comedienne," Carley said without humor.

She liked Reba. The girl had been born with a type of spina bifida. She had a dwarflike appearance and used a wheelchair. But she had an effervescent personality and a sunny disposition. She had been hospitalized for corrective surgery to her abdominal area.

"Once Kyle gets to know you, Carley, I bet he'll like you."

"I told you, guys don't like girls who look like me." She almost used the word *freak*, but stopped herself.

"Maybe dumb, immature guys. My dad says that beauty is in the eye of the beholder."

"Reba, get a grip. In the years between twelve and twenty, guys don't think with their brains. Or see with their eyes. They see through the eyes of all their friends. And of their friends' friends."

Reba laughed. "Well, maybe Kyle will be different. Maybe he'll like you for who you are."

"Sure . . . and if cows could fly, we'd all be wearing football helmets."

Afternoon sunlight filtered through the large window of Carley's room, which looked out on the expressways of the large city. Flecks of snow clung to the outside windowsill, and although it was the second week in January, faint smudges of the words *Merry Christmas* could still be seen on the inside of the glass.

Reba fiddled with the controls on her chair. "You've got to stop putting yourself down, Carley. Sure, your face is messed up, but at least you're alive."

"That's what my mother tells me," Carley said dryly. "It didn't help when I was twelve. It doesn't help now."

A nurse stuck her head through the doorway. "There you are," she said to Reba. "We've been looking everywhere for you. It's time for afternoon medications. Come on back to your room."

Reba made a face. "Do I have to?"

"Yes, you have to." The nurse stepped into the room and tugged at the wheelchair. "You can visit Carley later. Your doctor wants you on bed rest before your surgery."

"Go on," Carley told Reba. "I'll come down to your room after they deliver dinner."

When she was alone, Carley switched off the TV. She elevated the head of the bed until she was sitting upright, crammed the bed pillow against the small of her back, and sighed. She'd start physical therapy (PT) on her leg soon. The process would be painful, but she could endure it. No use having two parts of her body messed up. Yet it didn't seem fair to her that they could fix her leg but not her face. They could never fix her face.

Carley's phone rang. "Hey, Sis," the voice on the line said. "Are you driving the doctors and nurses nuts yet?"

"I consider it my sacred duty."

Janelle laughed. "Listen, Jon is driving me over tomorrow after school. I've got a *ton* of work from your teachers."

Carley had an instant image of her pretty eighteen-year-old sister and her boyfriend dragging in boxes full of homework. Today was Wednesday. "Don't they ever let up? I'm stuck in the hospital. Who has any energy to study?"

"Getting your leg healed and functioning again isn't a round-the-clock process," Janelle kidded. "I'm sure you can find an hour or two to hit the books. Oh, Mom said that she and Dad will be over Saturday morning to visit. Is there anything you want me to bring when Jon and I come?"

Carley was looking forward to seeing her

family. Her home in Oak Ridge was sixty miles from the hospital. With the distance to the hospital and everybody's work and school schedules, daily visits were hard to fit in. "Could you bring new batteries for my cassette player? And some more of my Books on Tape. They help pass the time."

"You should make friends while you're there. Don't clamp on that headset and ignore everybody."

"I'm in the hospital. How many friends can I make in a place like this?"

"You never know."

"Believe me, I know."

Just as Janelle hung up, the supper trays arrived. After eating, Carley went down the hall to visit Reba, whose room was full of relatives. Carley ducked away before anyone could see her and stare or ask questions. She hobbled back to her room as quickly as she could on her crutches. She watched TV and finally drifted off to sleep.

Carley awoke sometime in the night from a bad dream and lay wide awake, staring up at the ceiling. She couldn't recall the dream, only that it had left her heart pounding and her body damp with perspiration. She took slow, deep breaths to calm her heart but knew sleep wasn't going to return anytime soon. She decided to walk down the hall to the nurses' station at the far end. She was too antsy to stay in bed.

The corridor was quiet, and as usual for the night shift, it was dimly lit. She hopped out of her room and paused at the door to the room next to hers. It was the room of the boy Reba was so eager to meet, Kyle Westin. She wondered if he really was a hunk and where he went to school if he did live in Oak Ridge.

Carley didn't know why she nudged open his door. She saw in the dim light that Kyle lay in the bed, still turned toward the wall. Carley wondered if he'd even moved since his check-in. Was he paralyzed? she wondered. The night-light, mounted on the wall at the head of his bed, was on.

She edged closer, the rubber tips of her crutches squeaking. She realized she had absolutely no right to be in his room, but she stopped beside his bed and leaned over, hoping to catch sight of his face. Unexpectedly he flipped to his back and cried out, "Who's there? Who is it? What do you want?"

Carley was so startled, she dropped one crutch and attempted to hide her face with her open hand. She needn't have bothered. In the soft light she saw that large gauze pads covered Kyle's eyes. The pads were taped snugly to his temples and cheeks, and strips of gauze were wound around his forehead.

Kyle Westin couldn't see her. He was blind.

Two

"Who's there? What do you want?" Kyle repeated.

"Don't panic," Carley whispered hastily. "I—It's just me. I'm your neighbor. In the room next door. You know, a patient like you."

"What are you doing in my room?"

She didn't want to confess that she'd been acting nosy. "I thought I heard you make a noise as I was walking by toward the nurses' station. I was checking to see if you were all right."

He turned back toward the wall. "I'm not all right."

Nervously she chewed her bottom lip.

Leave, she told herself, but for some reason she couldn't. "Do you want a nurse? I could push your call button. I mean in case you couldn't find it since your eyes are bandaged." She felt stupid mentioning the very thing he was surely most sensitive about. She hated it when small children pointed at her and asked, "Hey! What's wrong with your face?"

"I don't want a nurse," Kyle said. "A nurse can't help me."

"Well, I'm sorry if I scared you." She bent down to pick up the crutch that had fallen, then repositioned it under her arm. "So, I'll just excuse myself—"

"What time is it?" He acted as if she hadn't spoken.

"Um—it's three o'clock."

"Is it afternoon already?"

"Three in the morning."

He rolled over to face her. "And you're out roaming around?"

Although his eyes were bandaged, Carley saw that light brown hair spilled over the tops of the gauze strips wound around his forehead to help hold the eye pads in place.

His cheeks were broad and high, his jaw square, his complexion smooth. He was as good-looking as Reba had hoped he'd be. "Couldn't sleep," Carley answered. "I had a bad dream."

"I can't sleep either."

Silence filled the room, yet Carley still couldn't make herself leave. He seemed so helpless, bewildered and lonely. She remembered when she was twelve, how terrified she'd been alone in the hospital. With doctors poking and prodding and machines and medicines that frightened her or made her sick. With pain in her face so intense, it had made her scream. "The nurse can give you something to help you sleep," Carley told Kyle kindly.

"I don't want to sleep."

She understood that part too. She, too, had once been afraid to fall asleep. Afraid that if she did, she wouldn't wake up. "Sometimes, it's best just to give in and take extra pain medication," Carley said. "It helps you stay mellow."

"Who said I needed pain pills?"

"Just a guess."

"I don't want any pain pills. I hate the way they make me feel."

"I know—like you're in 'la-la' land. Sort of dopey and spaced out. But sometimes that's not so bad because it helps make the time pass faster."

He kept turning his head, as if fixing on her voice. She stepped closer so that he wouldn't have to work so hard. "What's your name?"

Carley hesitated, then realized that to her he had form and substance, but to him she was only a disembodied voice floating in a dark void. He was blind. He couldn't see anything. She was safe. "Carley Mattea," she said.

"I'm Kyle Westin." Awkwardly he held out his hand. Too high, but she managed to reach and clasp his palm. He didn't let go. "You're right, Carley. I hurt a lot, but I don't want any pills."

"It's okay to take them when the pain's really bad."

"But I want to hurt."

"You do? Why?"

"Because the pain reminds me that I still have eyes."

Goose bumps appeared along her arms. The image of his strong male face without eyes unnerved her. "That's an odd thing to say. I figured you did. I mean, why wouldn't you? If you want to tell me," she added hastily. She hated to be asked about her scarred, lopsided face.

"Some friends and I decided to make our own rocket fuel. You know, just to see if we could. It exploded in my face. Burned my corneas and my chest." He pulled back his hospital shirt and she saw large bandages across his upper body.

She smelled ointments and cotton padding and winced, knowing how badly even a sunburn hurt. "Will the burns be all right?"

"They don't think I'll need skin grafts."

"That's good."

He paused. "But they're not sure if I'll ever see again."

She heard his voice catch and felt waves of pity for him. When she'd been younger, she'd suffered with headaches so severe that she'd passed out from the pain. And when the doctors had discovered a tumor in her left nasal cavity pressing against her brain, she'd had to have immediate surgery.

At the time, she'd overheard her parents talking in soft, frantic whispers to her doctor. They'd asked, "What's the worst that could happen?"

And he'd answered, "It could be malignant and she could lose the left side of her face."

She asked Kyle, "When will they know about your sight?"

"The eye specialist said that the corneas have to heal, and that can take two to three months."

"So you have hope. That's good."

He sank back against his pillow. "I don't feel real hopeful. I—I hate being blind."

By now Carley had settled herself on the edge of his bed in order to take the weight off her leg, which was throbbing. She knew what hopelessness felt like too. It was waking up from surgery knowing that she'd been cut across the top of her head from one ear to the other and down the front of her face. It was knowing that in order for the tumor to be removed, she'd had to lose parts of facial bones, which could never be replaced. It was learning that although her left eye and her mouth had been left intact, her face was permanently disfigured and scarred.

Feeling grateful that she wasn't blind, Carley said, "But you may still get your eyesight back. Don't give up."

Kyle took a deep, shuddering breath. "Yeah. Sure."

"So," she asked, "should I get lost now and let you try to get some sleep?"

His hand tightened on her wrist. "Don't leave. Please. I—It helps to talk."

"No problem." His hair looked soft and she wanted to touch it.

"Why are you in the hospital?" he asked.

"I got Rollerblades for Christmas and managed to fall and break my leg really bad. The doctor set it, but it wasn't healing just right, so they decided to operate and put the bones back together with pins and screws. That was two days ago, but when they got in there, I had an infection, so I have to stay in the hospital awhile. They dump antibiotics into me through an IV four times a day, but whenever I'm unhooked, I grab my crutches and wander around."

"Will your leg be all right?"

"Eventually, but I have to begin physical therapy soon, then come back for more once I check out and go home. I'll be glad to lose these crutches. I mean, I can't sneak up on *anybody*."

For the first time she saw him smile. "I think that's what I heard. The tips of your crutches squeaking. I guess it's true what they say about a person's other senses getting sharper when one of them is missing."

"Don't tell me that. I have a teacher who's deaf as a post and I sure don't want his eyesight any sharper. He may catch me reading the novel I prop behind the text for his class."

Kyle smiled again. "You're funny."

She wanted to tell him that her sense of humor was a by-product of living with her facial deformity, but then realized that there was no reason to divulge what he couldn't see. "A sense of humor helps," she said. "Laughing makes hurting less painful."

"So when I start hurting, I should find something to laugh about?"

"Well, there are degrees of pain. The very worst requires pain pills—a topic we've already covered. But the not-too-bad pain can be helped with a good laugh." She didn't add that *emotional* pain was a whole separate matter from the physical kind. Or that laughing and making jokes about her face over the years was her way of putting others at ease, no matter how much it hurt her.

She continued. "Think about it. Before your accident, you knew nothing about making rocket fuel. Now I'll bet you could write a term paper on how *not* to make the stuff."

She saw his expression work through the tragedy to the black comedy of his situation and was rewarded by his wry smile. "I see your point."

"And that's another thing. Do you know how many times we use the words *see* and *look* when we're trying to tell somebody something? Now you have the perfect excuse to say, 'No, dumbo, I don't see, and I can't look.'" She held her breath, hoping he wouldn't take offense, and was rewarded by another smile.

"What are you, a philosopher?"

"No way. I prefer art to philosophy."

"I used to prefer chemistry," he said.

She applauded. "Great, you're catching on already. 'Used to prefer chemistry'—get it? That's black comedy if ever I heard it."

"I won't let one feeble joke go to my head." He shifted in the bed, but hung on to her arm. "You like art. Do you draw?"

"Some. Mostly I like to design. You know, like clothes and fashion stuff. And I'd like to start with these stupid hospital gowns."

"So where do you go to school?"

She hesitated, not wanting to tell him. If they did attend the same school, it meant that he'd expect he might run into her in the halls if he ever got his sight back. And she knew she didn't want him to see her as she really looked.

Just then his room door opened and a nurse entered. She stopped stock-still and blinked at the two of them. "Good grief, Carley, what are you doing in this room at three o'clock in the morning?"

Three

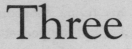

Carley scrambled off the bed and grabbed her crutches. "I couldn't sleep and came looking for company."

"Maybe other patients would like to sleep," the nurse chided.

"It's okay," Kyle interjected. "I asked her to stay and talk to me. I couldn't sleep either."

The nurse pursed her lips. "I don't think your doctors would approve of your late hours. It's time for vitals. Go back to your room, Carley, before we all get into trouble."

Vitals meant the process of taking blood pressures and temperatures, which the nursing staff did routinely round the clock. "I figured I'd save you the trouble of waking me up," Carley said, starting toward the door.

"Carley?" Kyle called out to her.

She turned. "Yes?"

"You were right about pain being easier to take if you laugh some. You've helped me feel better. Thanks for that. Will you come back and visit me in the morning?"

She felt her heart do a flip. No boy had ever expressed an interest in her. But then Kyle couldn't see how ugly she was. "If you want me to."

"Anytime," he said.

"Shoo," hissed the nurse at Carley good-naturedly.

Carley angled her way out the door, looking back to see Kyle raised up on his elbow. His white bandaged eyes were turned in her direction, as if she were the center of the universe and her return the most anticipated event in recorded time.

"You met Kyle in the middle of the night? That's just so cool! Tell me, what's he like?"

Carley wasn't prepared for Reba's visit. After she'd left Kyle's room, she had returned to her own and promptly fallen into a deep, dreamless sleep, which had ended at eight A.M. with the clanking arrival of breakfast trays. She was eating when Reba rolled into the room, but Carley was groggy and in no mood to play Twenty Questions. "He's had a chemistry accident and burned his eyes and he's not sure he'll get his sight back again. So he's not having a very good time," she mumbled between bites of soggy cereal.

"That's awful." Reba's eyes grew wide with sympathy. "Is he nice? Do you like him? Was I right—is he cute?"

"Slow down. My brain's only half awake."

Impatiently Reba nudged her wheelchair closer to where Carley sat on her bed with her tray table positioned over her lap. "Well, hurry and wake it up. They're taking me down for X rays soon."

Carley smiled at Reba's zealousness. "And I've got to go to PT at ten. Yes, he's nice. Yes, I like him. Yes, he's cute."

"Do you realize that this could be the start of a major relationship? And to think you met right here in the hospital."

"He was scared and alone last night. We

talked. But I don't think he's ready to make me his girlfriend."

"Well, I want you to introduce me to him. Will you do that?"

"Of course I will. But he's probably sound asleep, and besides, I'm sure he'll be here for days."

"Yes, but by this time tomorrow I'll be down in surgery, then in Recovery and ICU. It may be days before I'm up and rolling again."

Carley shook her head in defeat. "All right, let's go next door and pester Kyle."

She poked open his door cautiously, not wanting to wake him if he were sleeping. He was sitting up in bed patiently pressing the TV remote from channel to channel, pausing to listen for a moment before moving on.

"We're here to rescue you," she said, moving into his room and holding the door for Reba.

"Carley!" He sounded so pleased, it made her heart skip a beat. "Who's 'we'?"

"This is my friend Reba."

Reba rolled up alongside Kyle's bed and touched his arm. He groped with his free hand until he caught her hand. "I'm in a wheelchair," Reba said. "It's electric, so if you hear a whirring sound, you'll know it's me."

"I'm hearing sounds I never noticed when I could see."

Carley didn't want him to get depressed about his eyesight again, so she changed the subject. "Reba here is sort of the social coordinator of the floor, but she's got a date with her surgeon tomorrow and she didn't want you to get checked out before she recovered enough to be back on the job."

Reba giggled.

"I'm here for probably a week," Kyle said. "An ophthalmologist is keeping tabs on my eyes and another doctor keeps a check on my burns. As soon as they heal enough, I can go home."

"I hope it works out for you," Reba said.

"What about you? Will your operation get you out of your wheelchair?"

"No. They can't fix what's wrong with me. But the operation will make me more comfortable."

Kyle's expression was one of shock that

Reba couldn't be "fixed." Carley wondered how he would have reacted to Reba if he'd been able to see her. Or to Carley. She felt insulated and safe so long as he couldn't see either of them.

"I—I'm sorry." Kyle's fist balled up among the covers. "It's so frustrating not being able to see anything. I feel like a nonparticipant. I can't even get out of bed without someone to help me. I hate asking for help all the time."

"I can help out a little," Carley said. "If you want something—even company—call my room."

"I can't dial the phone."

"Sure you can." Carley came closer, picked up the phone, and placed it in his lap. "Take the receiver and feel the numbers pad." She watched his fingers trace over the raised buttons. "I'm in Room eight-twenty-eight, so you dial a seven plus eight, two, eight. Get a mental picture of how the pad looks and let your fingers locate the numbers. Now push them." She pressed his fingertips from number to number and dialed her room. "Each key has a different tone, you know. Pay attention and pretty soon you'll be able to dial area codes, seven-digit numbers, even foreign cities."

Gingerly he experimented, listening attentively to each electronic tone. He was rewarded by the sound of a phone ringing from next door. His face broke into a grin. "All right. I did it."

"A piece of cake," Carley said. "If I'm in my room, we'll talk. And if you want something, I'll come hopping over."

Kyle asked, "How do you know so much about dialing the phone 'blind' if you can see?"

"I can tell your parents have never put you on phone restriction." Carley patted his shoulder as if she were indulging a small child. "Why I've learned to slip this sucker under the covers at night, dial in the pitch-dark, and not misdial a single digit."

Reba clapped.

From the edge of Kyle's bed Carley performed a mock bow. "Thank you. Thank you."

Kyle laughed. "I can tell I'm in the presence of a true genius in devious maneuvers. I'm impressed."

Carley felt a twinge of guilt. Would he consider her failure to tell him about her scarred face devious? She gave Reba a sidelong glance, but Reba was looking raptly at Kyle, so it didn't seem as if she thought anything was amiss in Carley's purposeful omission.

"Did you know that you and Carley both live in Oak Ridge?" Reba blurted out.

"No. Why didn't you tell me, Carley?"

She felt her cheeks flush, then realized he couldn't see her embarrassment. She shot Reba a look that said, *Blabbermouth!* Reba shrugged innocently. "I was going to, but we got interrupted last night," Carley explained.

"Where do you go to school?"

Her heart began to pound. More than anything, she didn't want them to be students at the same high school. She took a deep breath and named her large public high school. "I started in September as a sophomore," she said. "But I don't do any after-school stuff—you know, clubs and things."

"I go to Webb." It was a prestigious private school. "I'm a junior. And I used to belong to the chemistry club."

Carley breathed a sigh of relief. At least that hurdle was crossed. "I'm sure your membership won't be revoked due to your mishap."

"And I go to middle school, but not in Oak Ridge," Reba offered, as if the only important information was their schools. For Carley the most valuable information was that she'd never have to meet Kyle in the halls and have him stare or, worse, turn his head away in distaste.

Two white-coated doctors and a nurse's aide swept into Kyle's room. "Good morning," one of them said, glancing at the three of them. Carley automatically dipped her head to allow her long brown hair to sheild the left side of her face. "Kyle, it's Dr. Goldston and Dr. Richmond. Are we interrupting anything? We've come to take you down to Ophthalmology and change your bandages."

"It has to be done in the dark," Kyle explained to Carley and Reba. "My eyes are real sensitive to light."

"We've got places to go." Carley assured him, hustling to pick up her crutches.

In the hallway Reba stopped her chair and said, "Kyle sure is nice. And good-looking too. It must be terrible to be blind. I feel sorry for him, don't you?"

"Of course."

"Well, I'm betting he gets his eyesight back," Reba said firmly. "Don't you think he will?"

"No way of knowing." Carley was aware that a small, perverse part of her was glad that Kyle couldn't see. She felt bad about it, but also knew that his blindness was her safety net. So long as he couldn't see her, he would think she was normal.

And for Kyle Westin, normal was what she wanted to be.

Four

Carley returned to her room, where she was hooked to an IV for her dose of antibiotics. By the time she was unhooked, it was time to go down to PT to begin rehabilitation on her leg. An aide took her down in an elevator in a wheelchair, along a covered walkway, to a separate building. Inside, a large and spacious physical therapy room was filled with equipment and tables. Therapists were working with patients of all ages.

"My name's Linda Gallagher and I'll be your PT." The woman who stood in front of Carley was slim and youthful, with long hair that hung down her back in a French braid.

"I'll be working with you twice a day thirty minutes per session in a series of exercises to get your leg functioning perfectly again. You'll be off those crutches in no time."

"What? Give up my crutches? How will I fight off my admirers?" Carley didn't bother to hide her face from the physical therapist. She figured the woman was used to seeing deformity.

Linda grinned. "So, I have a comedienne for a patient. Believe me, you're a welcome departure from the kind who grumbles all the time." She helped Carley out of the wheelchair, boosted her up onto a low table, and started examining her leg, which was held rigid by a cast. "What happened?"

Carley told her about the accident.

"And this was the day after Christmas?"

"Yes, but after I'd spent almost two weeks in the cast, X rays showed that it wasn't going back together just right, so Dr. Olson told us he'd have to operate and reset it."

"And, according to your chart, that's when they discovered the osteomyelitis."

"The what?"

Linda smiled. "The infection."

"Whatever. Anyway, I have to stay in the hospital until it goes away."

"It'll give us time to establish your therapy."

Carley kept waiting for Linda to ask about her misshapen face. Linda didn't. Instead she started right in explaining about the therapy. "We'll start with simple stretching exercises. Your chart states that you sustained tendon damage around your knee and ankle too."

"My doctor said he may have to operate on the tendons again." She understood the severity of her break and how concerned her parents had been about it. But considering her medical history, she refused to get too agitated about a broken leg. It would be fixed. However, she regretted losing her Rollerblades over it.

After the leg had been set the first time, her mother had said, "Those Rollerblades are going in the garbage."

Carley had protested, "But Mom, they're brand-new. I just got them!"

"I don't care. Don't you realize that because of them you could walk with a limp for the rest of your life?"

To which Carley had replied, "I'd look like Quasimodo in *The Hunchback of Notre Dame*, wouldn't I?" She leaned over, curled her lip, and dragged her leg which was now encased in plaster.

"That isn't funny, Carley," her mother said.

"Why not? Bum leg and weird face. I think it's funny."

Linda, the PT, interrupted Carley's thoughts. "You'll also start riding the stationary bike and in about ten days you'll begin partial weight-bearing exercises. I'll start you out with two-pound weights, take you to four, and eventually get you to where you'll once again have full ROM—that's range of motion."

"Will I be able to drive?" Carley had taken her road test in October, on her sixteenth birthday.

"Not right away," Linda said. "But it is your left leg, so if you've got an automatic shift, it shouldn't be too long before you can drive. Just be careful. You don't want to rack up the other leg."

"That's for sure. I hate being stuck in the hospital."

"We'll get you out as soon as we can," Linda said cheerfully.

Carley thought about Kyle, lying upstairs, a prisoner of his darkness. "Do you work with blind people?"

"No, I don't. But we have people on our staff who do. Why?"

"There's this guy on my floor who's blind, and I was wondering what you all did to help somebody like him."

"First his doctor has to authorize it, but basically, in the beginning, he'll have to be trained to move around safely. Plus he'll need to be counseled from a psychological perspective. Blindness is a big emotional adjustment."

Carley understood perfectly about adjusting to the emotional aspect of a catastrophic event. When she'd been told that the tumor removed from her face had been cancerous and that nothing could be done to reconstruct her lost bone and tissue, she'd gone into a deep depression. She'd wept for days, even though her doctor had tried to console her with the news that he'd cut out all of the tumor and that after chemotherapy treatments she shouldn't have to worry about the cancer ever returning.

At the time, they'd shaved her head, operated, and stitched her up so that black sutures ran in long lines over the top of her head and around her nose. With time, her hair grew back and the suture lines faded. But the deformity remained. Her face looked sunken on the left side, her nose scrunched, her eye half closed. She was ugly—no doubt about it.

"Well, I'm hoping his doctors can fix up this guy so that he won't be blind," Carley told Linda, forcing herself away from painful memories.

"I hope so too," Linda said.

Carley started her therapy thinking more about Kyle and his problems than her own broken leg. She wanted the best for him. She just didn't want to be in his line of vision when, and if, his bandages came off.

———

"Hi, Sis. Whatcha doing?" Janelle breezed into Carley's hospital room, shopping bags in each hand, her purse slung over her shoulder.

"Bowling."

Janelle laughed. "I see you haven't lost your sense of humor."

Carley was sitting in a recliner chair, her leg outstretched. She tossed down the magazine she was reading. "Where's lover boy?"

"Jon's coming; he stopped down at the snack bar." Janelle plopped the bags on the floor, leaned down, and hugged Carley, then grabbed another chair and pulled it closer. The bag tilted and spilled books onto the floor. "You've got homework in every subject."

"That brightens my day."

"Tell me what's happening. Mom and Dad want a full report."

Carley described her physical therapy session.

"Did it hurt?" Janelle asked.

"Like crazy. But you know what they say: No pain, no gain."

"Jon says that all the time."

"Remind me never to use that phrase again."

Janelle eyed Carley narrowly. "Be nice."

"Do I have to?"

"Why don't you like my boyfriend, Carley?"

Carley didn't know exactly how to answer. She hadn't meant to sound so caustic. She hedged. "Jon's okay."

Before Janelle could press for more of an answer, Jon walked into the room. He carried a sack from the snack bar in one hand and a giant cup of cola in the other. "How you doing?" he mumbled toward Carley, careful to avert his eyes from her.

"Doing just great," she said.

"You want to sit by us?" Janelle asked.

"No," he answered, much too quickly. "I'll just drag a chair over here." He indicated the small table on the other side of the room. "Mind if I turn on the tube?"

"Help yourself," Carley told him.

"I thought you came to visit." Janelle sounded irritated.

"You girls want to gab. I'll stay out of your way." He opened the sack and extracted a

hamburger, fries, and a pile of ketchup pack-
ets. He switched on the TV.

Janelle turned toward Carley and
shrugged. "I'm sorry. I thought he'd be more
sociable."

"I'm used to it."

"What's that supposed to mean?"

"Nothing. I'm just saying it's all right if he
does his own thing. He's *your* boyfriend. I
wouldn't expect him to get excited about
coming to the hospital to see me."

Janelle frowned as if she knew something
wasn't quite right, but since Jon was in the
room she couldn't make Carley talk about it.
"Have you heard from any of your friends
from school?"

"I don't have friends like you do, Janelle."

"What about that Dana girl?"

"We haven't been friends since Thanks-
giving."

"I didn't know that."

"When the guys started noticing her, she
dropped me like a hot potato."

"Well, that was mean of her."

Carley sighed. Janelle was wrapped up in
her own social life. Not that Carley blamed

her. Janelle was in her senior year and plan-ning on college. Plus, she was pretty and popular and outgoing. "I've forgiven Dana. Why should she be saddled with a social lia-bility like me?"

"She's petty. And you're *not* a liability."

"She's normal," Carley corrected.

"Well, have you made any friends here? A few days ago you were still groggy from your surgery, but surely you've poked around by now."

Carley told her about Reba and Kyle.

Janelle sucked in her breath when she heard that Kyle was blind. "I'd hate to think of a guy with his whole life ahead of him being blind," Janelle said.

"His blindness may not be permanent. His doctors aren't sure yet."

"That's a relief." Janelle tipped her chin forward and studied Carley thoughtfully. "Do you like him?"

"Of course I like him. Why wouldn't I?"

"No, I mean *like* him, like him."

Carley blushed under her sister's keen scrutiny.

"You do, don't you?"

"I hardly know him. We've had maybe two conversations."

"So what? I knew I liked Jon the first time I laid eyes on him."

"Well, Kyle's never laid eyes on me. And believe me, if I have my way about it, he never will."

Five

That evening Carley had just finished supper when her phone rang.

"It's me," Kyle said.

Her pulse fluttered crazily. "Hello, 'me.'"

"I dialed the phone just like you taught me. Got it right on the first try."

"I'd applaud, but I'm holding the receiver."

He laughed. "Doing anything?"

"Counting the flowers on the wallpaper."

"Want to come visit me?"

Her heart skipped a beat. "Sure. Let me grab my crutches and hop over." He wanted to be with her! She forced herself to calm down. After all, he was trapped in the hospital and didn't have anything else to do. Plus, he'd never seen her face.

She went to his room and found him sitting in a vinyl armchair at the small table in the corner of his private room. "You've made progress. You're out of bed."

"Yeah. You missed all the excitement. I spilled my lunch tray all over the floor. My mom was just walking in the door when it happened and she pitched a fit because no one was helping me. I told her that the nurses were busy and I shouldn't have gotten impatient. Besides, I don't like being fed like I'm some kind of baby."

Carley was sympathetic to his feelings. She said, "*Being* helpless and *feeling* helpless are different things."

"Exactly. Anyway, Mom nailed my doctor and he sent someone who works with the visually impaired to see me. She taught me some things about how to negotiate in a seeing world."

"Like what?"

"Come sit over here and I'll show you."

She watched him fumble for another chair. "I'll get it," she said.

"No." His voice was firm. "I need to learn how to handle things like this."

Slowly, he caught the arm of the second chair, stood, and pulled it out from the table. His movements looked choppy, but he did get the chair for her. She lay her crutches aside and sat down, propping her broken leg on another chair. "I'm impressed," she said. "The last time a guy pulled a chair out for me was in seventh grade."

She didn't add that it had been done as a cruel joke. As the boy had pulled it out, he'd turned to his buddies and said, "Freak alert." They'd all laughed and she'd felt humiliated.

"Okay, so I might not have offered if I wasn't trying to show off," Kyle admitted.

"I'm glad you've learned some things to help you take care of yourself. Nobody likes to feel useless."

"I guess you would understand."

"What do you mean?" She caught her breath. Had someone told him what she looked like?

"Your broken leg. I guess people are always rushing to help when you want to learn to do things for yourself."

She let out her breath slowly. "That's right. I've had to knock people over with my crutches in order to get them to let me do things for myself."

His brow furrowed, then he grinned. "You're joking."

"Must not have been much of one."

"It's just that it takes me longer to catch on to things because I can't see people's faces and read their expressions."

"I didn't think of that."

"This being blind is hard stuff. My doctors are saying that if the chemicals that burned my eyes were acids, then I have a good chance of recovering my sight. But if they were alkaline, I may never get it back."

"Don't you know what chemicals you used to make the fuel?"

"I've been trying to remember, but my friends and I were mixing lots of stuff that afternoon." He shook his head. "All I know is that I want to see again. I have to, Carley. I just *have* to."

She heard passion in his voice. She, too, had felt that same kind of longing. She craved to have a normal appearance, but no amount of wishing for it could restore her looks. Beauty was for other girls. It couldn't belong to Carley. "Well, until you can," she said cheerfully, "at least you'll know how to manage."

Kyle leaned back in his chair, his palms flat against the table. She wondered if touching something made him feel grounded, more connected. "One of the worst parts is being bored," he told her. "TV is a waste. I tried to listen to one of my favorite shows, but I couldn't make sense of it."

"I can see and I can't make sense of most of them."

He rewarded her attempt to lighten his mood with a smile. "I realized that a lot of the show's humor depended on visual gags, on the actors' expressions. Anyway, I had a hard time following, so I turned it off."

She had a sudden inspiration. "You need to borrow some of my Books on Tape. You have a cassette player, don't you?"

"Of course."

"Then I'll loan you some of my books."

"What kind of books?" He sounded skeptical. "Not romances, I hope."

"I have those, but I won't force them on you. I also have mysteries, thrillers, fantasies —in fact, if you have any lit books you need to read for school, I could probably find a few of those titles too. Sort of like Cliffs Notes for the ears."

He laughed. "How about chemistry and physics books?"

"Get a grip. I'm talking entertainment here, not instant tranquilizer."

"You wouldn't mind loaning me some of your tapes?"

"I offered, didn't I? You'll like them, and listening to them will take you right out of this place."

"You can't imagine just how much I'd like to be out of here."

She recalled wishing the same thing when she was going through her facial operation. Once they told her that removing the malignant tumor would leave her face deformed, all she wanted to do was run away, escape. She said to Kyle, "Don't you wish you had the power to turn back time? To go back to before your accident and start fresh and avoid the things that led up to it?"

"Yes," he said, his voice barely a whisper. "I can't believe how much you understand stuff, Carley. It's as if you can read my mind."

"It's easier to understand something once you've experienced it."

"You mean about your leg? Like you'd turn back the clock to before your accident and not do the same dumb stunt that led to breaking it?"

She was referring to her sense of loss over her looks, but of course he had no way of knowing about that. "Sure, I mean my leg. Who wants a broken leg with an infection in it?"

"And if I could start over with that rocket fuel, I would do things differently. I'd at least have put on safety glasses."

"Why don't you leave rocket-fuel con-cocting to NASA?"

"I will from now on."

She gazed at him in open admiration. Kyle was tall, good-looking, easygoing and, more than likely, popular—just the type of boy she'd always sneak peeks at in the halls at school. Just the type of boy who'd never notice her existence. Or worse, turn away in revulsion once he saw her face. But here, in the hospital, with his eyes bandaged, the scales of social acceptance were balanced. He couldn't loathe what he couldn't see. She could be at ease with what she couldn't change.

"Carley? Are you okay?"

She started. She'd been so deep in her thoughts, she'd almost forgotten they'd been in the middle of a conversation. "Whoops— sorry. I guess I had a temporary brain freeze. My mind wandered." She whistled, snapped her fingers, and called, "Here, mind, here, mind. Come back now."

Kyle broke into hearty laughter. "You're *so* funny. Most girls I know don't crack jokes like you do. Give me your hand."

"I'm still using it," she kidded, but held her hand out toward him.

He reached, caught her palm, and laced his fingers through hers. "There, that's bet-ter," he said.

She stared in fascination at their entwined fingers. "How do you mean?"

"I wanted to touch you. Hold on to you. You don't mind, do you?"

"No," she said, hoping the word hadn't tumbled out as fast as her heart had begun to beat. "I mean, it's fine with me."

"Can I ask you something personal?"

"How personal? My IQ is a closely guarded secret."

"Do you have a boyfriend?"

Caught totally off guard, Carley was momentarily speechless. No one had ever asked her that question before.

"Um—not really."

He grinned. "That's good."

She squirmed self-consciously before realizing that he couldn't see her discomfort. "How about you?" she asked boldly, not sure she wanted to hear his answer. "Any special girl?"

He shook his head. "Basically I'm shy," he said. "I can't ever get up the courage to talk to girls. My tongue gets all tied in knots and I come off sounding like a jerk."

She found his confession hard to believe. "You don't seem shy to me. You talk to me."

"You're different."

If only you knew how different, she thought. She asked, "So, what makes me different?"

"I don't know exactly. But when you wandered into my room and started talking to me, I knew you were different. You really understand what this is like for me . . . this . . . this being blind."

"I know it's got to be tough."

"My doctors keep preparing me for being impaired. And so did the woman who worked with me this afternoon. Even if my sight comes back, it probably won't ever be the same."

Carley didn't know what to tell him. She didn't want him to think his situation was hopeless, but she didn't want to ignore the seriousness of it either. "Well, don't dwell on the downside. Just work hard at becoming self-sufficient. It'll make waiting around for the outcome easier."

He squeezed her hand. "You have a way of saying the right thing to me." Suddenly he pushed back from the table. "What time is it?"

Carley glanced at the clock on the wall.

"Almost seven." She was amazed at how the time had flown since they'd been together. "Why?"

"My parents are coming any minute now. I want you to meet them."

Panic gripped her. She couldn't let them see her. "Oh, I can't." She grabbed for her crutches.

"But why not? What else is there to do around this place?"

She thought fast. "Reba," she said, struggling to her feet. "Remember, she's got surgery tomorrow and I've got to go visit her and make sure she's all right."

He nodded in understanding.

Carley bolted for the door, moving as fast as she could on her crutches, afraid to glance down the hall toward the elevators in case Kyle's parents might be headed her way. Afraid they might see the girl with the twisted face leaving their son's room and ask questions about someone he thought was normal.

Six

Carley didn't visit Reba because her friend's room was crowded with relatives. So she marked time in the visitor's lounge, keeping her head ducked so that her long brown hair would help conceal the left side of her face. When it was after nine o'clock, she cautiously returned to her room and quickly shut the door. She called Reba and said she'd be pulling for her during her surgery.

"You still friends with Kyle?" Reba asked. She'd been given medication to help her sleep and her voice sounded slurry.

"We talked for a couple of hours tonight."

"That's nice. Did you mention your face?"

"No way. I'm enjoying him thinking I'm a regular girl."

"Someday he might see you."

"Not if I can help it. Think about it. Once my infection clears up, I'll go home and he'll make friends with someone else. If he's even still here."

"So you won't see him again when he's out of the hospital?" Reba's voice drifted.

"No," Carley said. "I won't see or talk to him again." She paused, sensing that Reba was fading fast. "Go on to sleep," she told her. "I'll see you as soon as they put you back in your room."

" 'Honesty is the best policy,' " Reba mumbled.

"What?"

"My . . . grandfather says . . . that . . ."

Carley sighed. "I'm changing the policy. Good night."

She hung up and lay staring at the ceiling until the nurse came to hook her up for her evening dose of antibiotic. With her thoughts on Kyle, she drifted into a dreamless sleep long before the medicine was finished dripping.

The next morning Carley gave several of her Books on Tape to Kyle. "Can you stay?" he asked.

"I'm on my way to physical therapy." She was feeling guilty. Maybe Reba was right. Maybe she should tell him everything.

"Can we talk more later?"

"I don't want you to get sick of me."

"It's all right if I do. We're in a hospital."

The gauze pads concealing his eyes made it difficult to know if he was teasing. "It's a good thing I have a sense of humor," she offered cautiously.

He grinned. "I made a joke and you caught on to it. I'm getting better at this humor stuff, huh?"

"Don't let it go to your head, buster." She said goodbye and went out into the hall, where an orderly took her down in a wheelchair for her PT appointment.

Once her session was over, Carley returned to her floor and asked about Reba at the nurses' station. "She came through with flying colors," a nurse told her. "She's down in Recovery, and we expect she'll be sent up here by late afternoon. But no visitors except family today."

"No problem," Carley said, feeling greatly relieved that Reba had done so well.

"By the way," the nurse said, "your lunch tray's been delivered to Kyle Westin's room. He told us you knew all about it."

She didn't, but she faked it with the nurse and hobbled down the hall to Kyle's room. He was sitting at the table, his tray in front of him. Another covered tray had been placed on the table facing an empty chair. "Are you eating your lunch and mine too?" she asked.

"Carley! Come sit. I thought we could have lunch together. I had to make the nurse think you had preapproved the idea. Do you mind?"

How could she mind eating lunch with a guy like Kyle? "Your company's much better than that exercise lady on TV at noon." She propped up her crutches and sat down. "What is this stuff?" she asked, lifting the lid. "It looks like roadkill."

"It tastes all right. Soup's good."

She watched him encircle the soup bowl

with one hand, pick up the spoon, keeping it low, lean far over the warm bowl, and ladle soup into his mouth. She felt grateful all over again that she had her eyesight. "Not bad," she told him.

"The soup or my table manners?" he asked.

"The way you maneuver," she explained. "The soup's dreary."

He laughed. "I've been practicing hard at learning how to feed myself. Every meal, I spill less and less. You know I'm feeling brave if I got up the nerve to invite you to have lunch with me."

"You seem to have a knack for it. Feeding yourself, I mean."

"The therapist taught me to touch all the food first, position it on the tray so that I'd know exactly where everything was, and keep my hands low when I come at it. It works."

Fascinated, she watched him for another minute. She'd been taught that it wasn't polite to stare, and she hated it when people stared at her, but Kyle couldn't see her studying him, so she didn't think she was be-ing rude.

"I'm still not very fast at eating, though," he apologized. "It's made me realize how quickly I scarfed down my food before."

"Don't we all," Carley said.

"So how's Reba doing?"

"I hear she's doing fine, but it'll be an-other day before I check on her personally."

"What're you doing tomorrow?"

She stirred her fork through a gloppy mound of mashed potatoes. "Well, after I check out the Saturday morning cartoons, my parents are coming for a visit."

"They don't come during the week?"

"They would if I was in bad shape," Car-ley explained. "They own a bookstore in Oak Ridge and they put a lot of time into running it. It's hard for them to get away. But on Saturdays they have extra help." Carley didn't mention her sister to Kyle or that both of them worked there most week-ends, Carley almost always in the back un-packing and pricing stock. She didn't like working with the public because people stared and asked dumb questions. Once, a small child had seen her face and had screamed in fright.

"What's the name of the store?" Kyle asked. "I'll drop in when all this is behind me."

She didn't want him doing that. She had meant what she'd told Reba—once she was out of the hospital, she didn't want to run into Kyle again—whether or not he could see. The hospital acted as a safe harbor, a place where they were on equal footing. Reluctantly she told him the name of the store, telling herself that if he should ever drop by, she could have family or employees tell him she wasn't there. Soon he'd stop coming.

"Is that why you have so many Books on Tape?" Kyle asked. "Which, by the way, are pretty cool. I'm partway through a murder mystery."

"I get the tapes from the store, but I've always loved to read, so it's just another way to 'read' a book as far as I'm concerned."

"When I read, it's chemistry and physics. Quantum theory. Stuff like that."

"That side of my brain doesn't work,"

Carley said with a laugh. "I'm a total waste when it comes to math and science, but I guess you have a reason for that."

He nodded. "I want to attend MIT—Massachusetts Institute of Technology—and take up engineering and maybe someday work for NASA. The one thing I've always wanted to do was learn how to fly a plane. I have an uncle who owns a small plane. He operates a business flying around real estate agents and advertising banners."

"I've seen those signs. They say Eat at Joe's and stuff like that."

"He's busy during football season flying over UT stadium with ad messages. He takes me up with him sometimes. He's even let me man the controls." Suddenly he grew quiet. "I want to be a pilot. At least I did. Until this happened."

He sounded so despondent that Carley was sorry she'd opened the door to the conversation. "I want to go to the Chicago Art Institute," she inserted quickly, hoping to get his thoughts off his situation. "Who knows, maybe I'll shake up the fashion industry with my 'innovative designs.'" She emphasized the last to make it sound comical, like words from a TV commercial.

"I'd ask to see your work, *but* . . ." Kyle said without humor.

Carley regretted her remark. Trying to cheer him up had backfired. "It's not much to see, really. Let's talk about something else."

"Why not? Talking seems like all I can do."

She stabbed her fork into a piece of chocolate cake on her food tray. "We could talk about dessert," she said. "It's chocolate and maybe older than both our combined ages."

He offered a half smile, but pushed his tray away. "I'm not hungry anymore. Everything's cold by now anyway."

"It's because I got you to talking instead of concentrating on lunch."

"It's because I'm blind," he blurted. "It isn't fair!" He shoved the tray again, and Carley had to grab at it to keep it from skidding off the table.

"I—I'm sorry," she said softly. He was breathing hard and she wasn't sure if he might want to cry. "I know it isn't fair, but sometimes we just have to live with what can't be changed."

"How would you know? All you have is a broken leg. Bones heal."

Of course she couldn't tell him how she knew. "I should be going," she said, reaching for her crutches. "Time for my afternoon antibiotic hookup."

He said nothing.

She headed for the door, the rubber tips of her crutches squeaking on the floor. She paused at the doorway and gazed back at him. "Bye."

"Bye," he said without moving.

Brilliant afternoon sunlight played across his golden brown hair and spilled across his gauze-bandaged eyes. But she knew that inside the bandages, he was alone in the dark. And there was nothing she could do about it. Not one single thing.

Seven

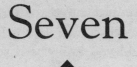

On Saturday morning Carley's parents came to visit, laden with a bag of books and tapes. "Your doctor says you'll probably be out of here early next week," her father said after kissing her on the forehead. "He says you're responding well to the antibiotic, and according to your X rays, your leg looks to be knitting properly."

"Good. I'm ready to blow this place." Carley joked, but she knew she'd miss Reba and Kyle. Most of all Kyle.

"Of course, you'll still have to come in for physical therapy," her mother said. "But that can be as an outpatient."

"My therapist seems to think I can drive,

so I can bring myself in for the sessions. No need for you or Dad to take off from work."

"Janelle can bring you."

"Sure—my sister's going to cut into her social life to usher me to therapy three times a week." Carley was thinking about Janelle's red-hot romance with Jon.

"She can just rearrange her priorities," Carley's mother said. "Your leg is more important than any of her extracurricular activities."

"Mom, it's no big deal," Carley insisted. "I can drive myself."

"We'll cross that bridge when we get there," her father said. "No use arguing about it now. Let's get you out of the hospital and home first."

Carley shrugged. Her dad was right. Why argue now? There was plenty of time to argue later. "So, how are things at the store?"

"Well, we're gearing up for Valentine's Day," her mother said. "We rearranged our magazine racks to make room for a line of greeting cards. I figure they'll sell really well. You know how business is: We start on back-to-school the first of August, fall merchandise in September, Christmas by October—"

"Even earlier these days," her father interjected.

"Anyway," her mother continued, "I'm redoing some displays with lots of red and white ribbons and lace and cute little Victorian-style cupids. And some of the romance publishers are putting out special Valentine titles, so we've got plenty of new displays with the holiday theme."

"My favorite holiday," Carley muttered unkindly under her breath.

"Valentine's Day is a wonderful holiday," her mother said, glancing at her husband, who gave her a wink.

Sure, Carley thought. *If you're normal.* Frankly she'd always thought some sadist invented it. Valentines and syrupy sentiments of love were a cruel joke. She'd learned early on that Valentine cards only went to pretty, popular girls. Janelle practically waded hip deep in them every year. "The best thing about Valentine's Day is that boxes of chocolate are half price on the day after," Carley said.

Her father laughed. "I see you haven't lost your wit."

"I don't want to be witless," she quipped, making him laugh again.

Her parents stayed until late afternoon, then hugged her goodbye and left. Once they were gone, Carley felt blue. She liked her family and she considered herself fortunate to have such supportive parents. All during her ordeal with the cancerous tumor, they had been by her side, and when she'd been permanently disfigured, they'd sent her to counselors and did everything possible to help her adjust to her lifelong disfigurement and build up her self-esteem.

She was deep in thought, when someone rapped on her door.

"It's open," she called.

Kyle entered her room, feeling his way cautiously along the wall as he went.

She scrambled toward him, wincing in pain over the sudden movement, but fearful that he might bump into something. "Let me help," she blurted.

"I can manage," he said. "Just tell me if anything's in my path."

"My room's exactly like yours," Carley told him. "Just flip-flopped." She watched him inch closer. "Does a nurse know you're trying to navigate on your own?"

"I didn't think I needed a guide. Or a red-tipped cane just yet."

Eventually he made it to the small table near her window, where he groped for a chair. She itched to help him, but sat quietly, since she knew he wanted her to. When he was finally seated, she let out a deep breath. "You're here," she said.

He grinned, his expression looking pleased. "Maybe I'm not so helpless after all." He rubbed his shins. "A little black and blue maybe, but not helpless."

"To what do I owe the honor of this visit?"

"I wanted to apologize for the way I acted yesterday."

"You were angry. I understood."

"I didn't have to take it out on you."

"I didn't take it personally . . . honest."

He shifted in his chair and leaned forward, holding out his hand in a gesture that asked her to take hold of it. Heart pounding, she slid her hand into his. "I—I think you're a really nice person, Carley. I can't imagine how I would have made it these past days without your help."

"That's me. Carley the Helpful One. How do you suppose that translates in Chinese?" She was babbling, but couldn't stop herself. She felt totally flustered by his sincerity. Absolutely unsettled by his attention.

"Um—I'd really like to ask you something."

"You can ask."

"I don't want you to think I'm weird or anything."

"This must be serious." She tried to sound lighthearted, but her palms were sweating. She hoped her hand didn't slip out of his.

"Not too serious." He tipped his head and his brown hair spilled over the gauze wrapped around his forehead. "I've just been wondering what you look like, that's all. I mean, you know what I look like and I haven't a clue as to what you look like."

Her heart wedged in her throat. How

should she answer him? "I look like a girl," she finally said. "Hair, arms, legs—the usual stuff."

He laughed, but she hadn't meant it to be funny. She didn't want to be discussing her looks with him. A sudden thought unnerved her. What if one of the nurses had alluded to the fact that she was less than perfect-looking? That something was wrong with her?

"But tell me about yourself. Are you tall, short, athletic? What color's your hair and your eyes? I'm not trying for your vital statistics, just a mental picture."

"Well. . . ." She drew out the word, stalling for time. "What do you think I look like?"

"That's not fair. No matter how I describe you, you can agree or disagree, whether it's true or not."

"I won't. Tell me, what's your mental image of me?"

He squirmed, and she knew she'd put him on the spot. But he'd put her on the spot too. "All I have to go on is your voice."

"How does my voice make me sound?"

"Your voice makes you sound friendly.

And nice." He appeared more comfortable with this third-person approach—this pretense that her voice was a separate personality.

"And what about the color of my hair? Can my voice give you a clue about that?"

"Blond?"

"Dark brown."

"Straight?"

"Like a board."

"Long?"

"Long," she confirmed. "And what color does my voice say my eyes are?"

"Um—blue."

"Brown."

"I like brown eyes. My favorite color." He grinned gleefully, caught up in the game.

"Oh, puh-lease . . ." she drawled dramatically.

"You don't believe me? It's true. In the first grade I had a crush on a girl named Trianna Lopez. She had the most beautiful brown eyes."

"Fine. Sit there and talk about another girl in front of me." Carley pretended to be miffed.

She didn't fool him. Kyle laughed and said, "She was only six!"

"I forgive you."

"I'll bet you're tall."

"Only five foot three. I'd never make the basketball team."

"That's all right. I've never had a thing for jocks." He toyed with her fingers still nestled in his hand. "I'll bet you're thin too."

"Average."

"There's nothing average about you, Carley."

She felt her face blush crimson. If only he knew how *un*average she really was. "So now are you satisfied? Do you have a picture of me?"

"Sort of."

"Well, here's what I've learned about *you*, mister," she said, poking him playfully with her forefinger. "You're attracted to tall, willowy blondes with blue eyes and straight hair. I, on the other hand, am a not-so-tall brunette with brown eyes and straight hair."

"One out of four isn't bad for a guy in my situation," he insisted.

For a second she thought he might get melancholy remembering that he was blind. Quickly she said, "All right, one out of four is good."

He sat still, his face turned fully toward her. For an eerie moment she thought he might be able to see through his bandages. "What now?" she asked.

"There's another way I could satisfy my curiousity a little bit. If you're willing, that is."

"How?"

"You could let me touch your face. You know, explore it with my fingers."

Eight

Kyle wanted to touch her face. But if he did, he'd know for certain something was wrong. Carley got an instant picture of his fingers tracing along the caved-in area between her left eye and nose and recoiling in horror. He'd ask, *"What's wrong with you?"* and she'd have to tell him that she was a freak. That just like Humpty Dumpty, all the plastic surgeons and medical geniuses couldn't put Carley Mattea back together again.

"I know you're still here," Kyle said, "because I'm still holding your hand. What's wrong? Did I upset you?"

"No," she said, a little too quickly. "I had

a shooting pain in my leg. I was gritting my teeth until it went away."

With those words Carley realized that she'd crossed a subtle barrier. Before, she'd simply avoided telling him the truth by not divulging certain details. Now she'd told him two outright lies. Truthfully she *was* upset, and there was no pain in her leg.

"I'm sorry," he said. "I thought maybe I'd offended you by asking to touch your face. I don't know why I asked. Maybe because the woman from blind services encouraged me to explore the world with my sense of touch. She said it would help me 'see' things. Forget it."

"It's all right. I—I really don't mind." *Another lie!* "But you know what I think would be better?"

"What?"

"I think it would be better to wait until you can actually see my face for yourself. Yes, that's what I want. I want to greet you face-to-face once your bandages come off."

He didn't say a word right away. He only held her hand and brushed his thumb repeatedly across her knuckles. "Even when the bandages come off, there's no guarantee I'll be able to see again."

"But I think you will," she insisted. "And because I think so, I want you to wait until you can see me with your own eyes."

"And if I can't?"

"Then you can touch away."

He slumped back in the chair.

She disliked bringing Kyle's mood from happy to glum; it wasn't a nice way to treat him. But she'd been desperate to take his mind off the idea of exploring her face with his touch. What a disaster it would have been. She didn't understand why it was so important to her that he maintain his illusions about her looks, but it was.

"Do you know what?" she asked brightly. "The orderly will be here any minute to take me down to PT." She told him another lie. She wasn't scheduled for another PT session until Monday morning.

"I'll go back to my room." Kyle stood.

"Let me walk with you."

"How? You're on crutches, remember?"

"We'll manage."

"Then let me take your elbow and follow

about a half step behind. That's the way I was taught to have someone lead me."

Carley let him grasp her right elbow and slowly she began to take small steps with her crutches so that he could keep up. Back in his room again, he climbed into the bed. "I think I'll listen to another one of those books you loaned me. I'm not much good at doing anything *but* listening."

"I have more," she said, eager to make up for any distress she might have caused him. "Mom and Dad brought me a bunch of new ones today."

"Will you come visit me later?" he asked.

"Absolutely."

"My parents are coming this afternoon. I'd like for them to meet you."

"Um—all right," she declared, knowing full well that she'd find something to keep her busy and away from her room so that she wouldn't have to meet them.

Carley returned to her room, grateful to be out of her awkward situation. How had she gotten herself into this mess? Was it wrong of her to want to protect herself from his discovering what she really looked like?

Was it wrong to want him to believe that she was normal, even pretty?

Later, when she figured Kyle's parents might be on their way up, Carley went to visit Reba. The girl was still recovering from her surgery, but fortunately she was alone in her room. IVs hung by her bed, and tubes leading from her stomach were partially concealed by bedcovers.

"For drainage," she explained to Carley.

"Are you in pain?" Carley might have felt revulsion if she hadn't been through so much medical trauma herself.

"Not much," Reba said. Her voice sounded soft and she spoke slowly, but at least she was lucid. She nodded toward a small machine next to her bed with its IV line threaded into her arm. "Morphine dispenser," she said. "If I start to hurt too bad, I can make the drip come faster."

"How long before you're able to get up?"

"Don't know." Reba's eyes closed, but soon opened again. "Talk to me. Take my mind off this stuff."

Carley told her about Kyle's visit and him wanting to touch her face.

"Wow," Reba mumbled. "Close call."

"Tell me about it. It's getting harder and harder to keep my secret."

"What if he asks one of the nurses about you?"

"Don't think I'm not worried about it. But they're professionals. So if one does tell him about me, I hope she'll be kind and won't say, 'Carley? You mean the dog-faced girl?' "

Reba grimaced. "No one would ever say that about you."

"You're wrong, Reba. Someone did say it."

"Who?"

"Jon, my sister's boyfriend."

"That's so mean!"

Carley patted Reba's arm. "Don't get worked up about it. It happened months ago. I was cutting through the gym at school and I heard some guys talking and heard one of them mention Janelle's name. Naturally I stopped and eavesdropped. They were telling Jon how lucky he was to have a babe like Janelle for a steady date. And too bad she didn't have a sister. And Jon said, 'She does —it's Carley, the dog-faced sophomore girl.'

"Then I heard a couple of the guys make

barking noises and Jon say, 'Man, I can hardly stand to look at her, she's so ugly.' I stopped listening then. I ran out of there as fast as I could. I didn't cry until I got home, but to this day I can't stand to be around Jon."

Reba's eyes grew wide as Carley talked. "Did you ever tell your sister?"

" 'Course not. It's too babyish to whine about it to her. I mean, what am I going to say? 'Your boyfriend called me a dog. I think you should dump him.' I need to be tough, Reba. Kids are always saying mean things about me. Dumb things. They don't know what it's like to look at this face in the mirror every day. People who are normal haven't got a clue about how badly words hurt. Worse than rocks sometimes."

Reba nodded. "Why can't people understand that no one likes being different. But people who are different still have feelings."

Carley realized that Reba, most of all, understood what she was saying. All her life Reba would be confined to a wheelchair. She was simply somebody that medical science couldn't make normal. A lump of tears lodged in Carley's throat. Tears for Reba. Tears for herself.

"I've been trying to figure out why I've let this whole thing with Kyle get out of hand," Carley said slowly. "I mean, why didn't I just come clean with him from the beginning? You told me to." Tears swam in her eyes.

"What do I know?" Reba offered a smile.

"You knew more than me. I guess it was just so nice to have a boy *like* me. And he liked me in spite of the way I looked. And now I can't seem to stop pretending with him."

"You could if you wanted to."

Carley shook her head. "No. I don't want to. I keep thinking that soon I'll get out of here and get back to my life."

"But once he gets out, he might come looking for you."

"But if he can't ever see me, it won't matter."

Reba blinked. "Do you hear what you're saying, Carley? It's almost as if you don't want him to get his eyesight back again."

Carley bowed her head. What Reba had said was true. She dreaded Kyle regaining his vision. And yet it was wrong to wish him confined to a lifetime of darkness simply because she didn't want him knowing she was disfigured. "He's the first guy who's ever been nice to me, Reba. The *only* one since before I was twelve."

"And you don't think he'll be nice to you once he knows what you look like?"

"No," Carley said miserably. "I live in the real world. And in the real world guys don't stick around for girls who look like me."

Just before bedtime Carley's phone rang.

"Where were you tonight?" Kyle's voice sounded hurt. "I told you my folks were coming and that I wanted you to meet them. Why did you run off?"

"I went to visit Reba. I hadn't seen her since her surgery and I didn't want her to think I'd forgotten about her," she explained quickly.

"Oh." His voice lost its edginess. "How she's doing?"

"Pretty good."

"Carley, I didn't mean to sound off at you. It's just that I've been talking about you to my friends and parents a lot. I've been telling them about this terrific girl I've met and they want to meet you too. Except that you're never around, so everybody thinks you're a figment of my imagination. Or worse, that I'm a liar."

Recalling Reba's admonition to come clean with Kyle, Carley took a deep breath. "Kyle, I think we should talk. I need to tell you something."

"Can you tell me tomorrow? The nurse just gave me a sleeping pill," he said, stifling a yawn.

"Sure . . . tomorrow's fine." She felt relieved. She really didn't want to confess everything tonight.

"Listen, my two best friends are coming tomorrow afternoon and I want them to meet you."

She wondered if this fetish of his to introduce her to his friends and family was ever going to end. "You're putting me on the spot, Kyle."

"Why? Just because I want my friends to meet the person who's making this whole ordeal bearable for me?"

She didn't know what to tell him and she didn't want to argue about it on the phone either. "We'll talk about it tomorrow."

"Tomorrow," he said, sounding drowsy. "But I promise we'll be next door to see you, so don't run off. Because if you do, we'll go looking for you if we have to search every floor of the hospital."

Nine

"You want *what*? Are you out of your mind?"

Carley bit her lip, not wanting to lash out at Janelle, who stood in the hospital room wearing an incredulous expression. "Don't get all hyper on me," she said as soothingly as possible. "I'm not asking you to rob a bank or anything."

"It's a dumb idea, Carley, and I won't do it. I won't pretend to be *you!*"

Janelle's stubborness was testing Carley's patience. Didn't her sister realize that she was desperate? And that desperate times called for desperate measures?

Carley had come up with the scheme late

the night before and called Janelle first thing Sunday morning. "Please come see me right away," she'd begged. "Don't even go to church first, just come straight here."

But when Janelle arrived and Carley revealed her plan for what she wanted Janelle to do later in the afternoon, Janelle adamantly refused. Carley glared at her sister, whose chin jutted out obstinately. "I never ever ask you for a favor, and the one time I do, you act as if I asked you to murder somebody."

"This is more than a favor, Carley. It's an out-and-out lie. I can't pretend to be you just so that you can impress some boy."

"This isn't some stupid kid prank, you know. I have good reasons for Kyle's friends to think that you're *me*. Kyle and I've become good friends. I really like him and I don't want his friends to tell him that I'm some kind of freak."

"You're not a freak!" Janelle stamped her foot. "And if anyone says you are, I'll deck 'em."

"Thanks for the show of loyalty." Carley sighed. "But I can deck people if I choose to.

The one thing I can't do is look normal. You're my sister and I need you to help me out here."

"You really like this guy?"

Carley nodded vigorously. Was her sister about to cave in?

"Then be honest with him. Tell him about yourself; he'll understand."

Carley exploded with "That's easy for you to say. You've never had people stare at you. Or call you names. Don't you see? I don't want to take the chance that he'll 'understand.' I want him to think I'm pretty. And if his friends meet *you*, then that's exactly what Kyle will think."

Unable to look Carley straight in the eye, Janelle sagged into a nearby chair and glanced down at the floor. "This is emotional blackmail."

"No. It's a favor. From one sister to another."

Suddenly Janelle sat upright, a gleam in her eye. "There is this small thing of your broken leg. Or do you expect me to throw myself down the stairwell?"

"I've already thought about that," Carley

said, holding up her hand. "If you roll into Kyle's room in a wheelchair with your leg stretched out and a blanket over your lap, no one will know that your leg isn't broken. Kyle's friends will see a pretty girl who says that her arms were hurting from using crutches. And Kyle won't see anything at all. I'm telling you, Janelle, this will work if you put a little effort into it."

"What will work?"

Both girls whipped around in the direction of the voice that had interrupted their discussion.

"Jon!" Janelle jumped up from the chair and went toward him. "What are you doing here?"

"I got to church and your mother said you'd come here instead, so I left and came looking for you. What's up?" He avoided looking at Carley.

Carley groaned and flopped back onto her pillow. Just what she needed—Jon to muddy up her plan. And just when she'd almost had Janelle persuaded.

"What's up is that my sister has some

harebrained idea about me impersonating her for this guy she's met in the next room."

Jon looked confused.

"He's temporarily blind," Carley interjected, none too kindly. "So he's never seen my face, and most likely never will. But his friends are coming to visit him this afternoon and he wants them to meet me and see what a 'babe' I am. But we all know that's not the case, don't we?"

Jon's face colored, but he still shook his head. "I don't want any guy coming onto my girl." His arm snaked around Janelle's waist possessively.

"Oh, puh-lease. . . ." Carley rolled her eyes dramatically. "Think of it as a temporary loan."

Even Janelle looked exasperated with him. "Cut the Neanderthal routine, Jon. I'm a person, not your property."

"But you're *my* girl!"

"And Carley's my sister."

"You're not seriously thinking about doing this, are you?" Jon sounded angry.

"What if I am?" Now that Janelle was on

the defensive, Carley decided to keep quiet and let the two of them argue it out. Maybe Jon's attitude was just the push Janelle needed to send her into Carley's camp on this issue.

"Because it's dumb, that's why."

"Yes, it's dumb, but Carley *is* my sister, and she wants my help."

"If she asked you to jump in front of a moving car, would you do it?"

"That is so lame. Just the kind of thing you'd tell a two-year-old. Which I'm not!" Janelle whirled around and started for the door. "I'm going to buy myself a Coke. Cool off, Jon!"

She grabbed her purse and flounced out the door. Jon glared after her.

"Not much fun to be called names, is it?" Carley asked him when they were alone.

Jon gave her a sullen glance and crossed to the window, where he stood with his hands thrust into his pockets and scowled.

Carley sat forward and swung her legs over the side of the bed. "It wouldn't kill you to cooperate, you know. We're talking a fifteen-minute visit that won't mean anything to you, but will mean everything to me. And to Kyle."

"It's just not right," Jon answered.

"Lots of things happen that aren't right. Like getting cancer when you're twelve and turning into a permanent sideshow. You know, someone's idea of a joke."

"What's that supposed to mean?"

"*Woof-woof.*" She saw the back of his neck and ears flush red. He turned slowly and their gazes locked. "I'm sorry you don't like me," she said. "But I can't help the way I look. And I don't like people making fun of me."

"Who says I don't like you?"

"It's written all over your face every time you look at me. Or rather, *don't* look at me."

She was surprised when he said, "I really care for Janelle. She means everything to me. Are you going to ruin it for us?"

Carley felt a sense of power and for a minute wanted to see him squirm, but the feeling passed when she remembered how urgently she needed Janelle's help. No use causing a scene simply to get revenge. "Wrecking people's lives isn't my style," she told him. "But I would appreciate a good word from you. It would help this deal go down much more easily."

Before he could respond, Janelle swept back into the room, a can of diet cola in her hand. "The vending machine hardly had anything good," she grumbled.

Jon took a deep breath and stepped in front of her. "I've been thinking while you were gone."

Carley resisted the urge to blurt, *"That's what you smell burning—Jon's brain."*

"I think you should help Carley."

Janelle glanced from Jon to Carley and back again to Jon. "I was gone less than ten minutes. How did she persuade you so quickly? Especially when she's been working on me for an hour."

"I overreacted. What she wants is really sort of harmless." He glanced toward Carley. "Sort of like wearing a mask for Halloween. This guy will be happy. Carley will be happy. No one will know it's you. And then that's the end of it."

Carley ignored Jon's bad humor and nodded eagerly. "I told you, Sis, it'll only take a few minutes, and you don't ever have to do it again."

Janelle's shoulders drooped. "I hate it when people gang up on me. Especially people I care about."

Carley felt a twist of guilt and vowed she'd make it up to her sister sometime. "I'll be grateful forever."

Her phone rang and she grabbed the receiver. It was Kyle. "Hi," she said cheerfully.

"You're in your room."

"You sound surprised."

"You usually run off."

"Now, now," she chided.

"Listen, my friends Steve and Jason are here. They were cohorts in my infamous rocket-fuel stunt, except that they didn't get hurt. Anyway we want to come by and say hello."

"Don't do that!" Carley cut her eyes to Janelle and Jon, tucked the receiver beneath her chin, and pointed frantically at the wheelchair she'd confiscated earlier from the nurses' station. "What I mean is, why don't I come to your room? It's a mess here and I don't want strange boys around." Janelle rolled her eyes. "I can be there in five minutes," Carley added, ignoring her sister.

"Sure, no problem," Kyle told her. "Come soon."

"I can't stay long," she warned. "I have visitors coming too, and I want to be in my room when they arrive."

"No problem. Stay ten minutes. Stay an hour. I only want my friends to meet you." She heard a smile in his voice. "I only want them to meet the most special girl in the whole world."

Ten

"I really hate this," Janelle whispered as Jon helped her into the wheelchair.

Carley limped over with a blanket from off the bed. "But I need you to do it so much. And I'll never forget how you helped me. I'll be grateful forever!" She pumped up the area with a pillow and tossed the blanket across Janelle's lap.

Jon leaned down and adjusted the footrest so that Janelle could prop her leg in a thrust-out position. "You know how to work one of these things?"

"I can manage," Janelle snapped.

Carley fussed with the blanket, making

sure that it covered Janelle's lap and leg completely. "Just tell him—"

"I know what to say." Janelle pushed herself toward the door, paused, and scowled back at Carley and Jon. "What about my voice? Do you think he's clever enough to hear a difference?"

Carley's stomach constricted. She'd forgotten about her voice. "You can do a pretty good imitation of me. You always did when we were little and you wanted to get me in trouble with Mom."

"We've grown up since then. At least, one of us has."

Carley gritted her teeth. Janelle certainly wasn't being agreeable. "You're going to do just fine," she said. "And you'll never know how much this means to me. Never, ever."

Janelle rolled out into the hall while Jon and Carley peeked around the doorframe. When Janelle knocked on Kyle's door, Carley ducked backward. "She's in," Jon said. "Now what?"

"Now we loiter in the hall by his door and maybe we can hear something."

Jon looked at her as if she were nuts, but he tagged along when she hopped out on her crutches. She rested her back on the wall beside Kyle's door, and Jon leaned his shoulder against the wall next to her. She strained to hear through the slightly ajar door, but only snatches of words and mumbles came to her. She whispered, "I sure wish I could hear better."

Jon arched his eyebrow at her. "If only we'd thought to put a tape machine in her lap, she could have gotten the whole conversation."

She flashed him a hateful look. All at once her knees started shaking as it dawned on her that she was manipulating people's lives! She was working so hard to protect *herself* that she was forcing her sister and her sister's boyfriend to conform to her will. And she was deceiving Kyle and his friends by misrepresenting herself to them. She felt a wave of guilt and remorse. And fear. If Kyle found out about her now, he really would hate her. And she couldn't blame him. But she felt as if she'd gone so far with her charade that she couldn't drop it now. She couldn't tell him the truth at this stage.

Kyle's room door swung open and Janelle rolled out in the wheelchair, waving good-bye over her shoulder. Carley ducked under Jon's arm and headed in the opposite direction down the hall, fearful that one of Kyle's friends might stick his head out the doorway and see her. When she felt it was safe, she returned to her room. Janelle and Jon were preparing to leave.

She shut the door fast. "So what happened?"

"Nothing happened. I was charming and sweet."

"Did Kyle say anything?"

"He said he'd call me later." Janelle picked up her purse and slipped on her coat. "But of course, he thinks I'm *you.*"

"You don't have to leave yet. We could watch an NBA game on TV, or maybe some old movie." Now that the charade was over, Carley didn't want to be left alone. She wanted her sister to stay. She wanted to get back into Janelle's good graces.

"I've got a Lit test tomorrow and I need to study for it." Janelle started for the door with Jon.

"Janelle," Carley called. "Thanks."

Janelle didn't smile. "You're welcome. We'll walk down the stairwell to the ground floor," she said. "Less chance of being seen by Kyle's friends."

Then Janelle and Jon were gone and Carley was alone. All alone.

"My friends were suitably impressed." Kyle was eating dinner in Carley's room. Their trays were spread out on the small table near the window, and the TV played softly in the background.

"That's nice," Carley said, grateful that he couldn't see how little she was eating. She didn't have much of an appetite tonight.

"What did you think of them?"

She started. Why hadn't she pressed Janelle for more details? "They seemed nice."

"Nice?" Kyle cocked his head. "Steve practically fell over your chair. Did he hurt your leg?"

"No. I'm fine."

"Is anything wrong?" His expression looked puzzled.

"No. Why do you ask?"

He touched his meat loaf, gave the plate a small turn, and cut off a piece with his fork. Carley realized he'd become quite adept at feeding himself despite his blindness. "You— um—sounded funny today."

"Funny ha-ha or funny peculiar?" She tried to laugh off his observation, but her heart began to thud.

"I don't know. Your voice sounded different to me this afternoon. Not like your usual self. I've grown used to your voice and the way it sounds. I like it."

"How does my voice sound?"

"Sort of sexy."

She giggled with pure pleasure. Her voice was hers alone, and he liked it. She didn't have to speak through her sister's mouth. It was Carley's voice Kyle heard. "Sexy? Me?"

"That's what I said." He grinned. "When all you have is someone's voice to go on, you notice the smallest change. And today you just didn't sound like yourself."

"Um—I had a little allergy attack right before I came by to see you. Maybe that made me sound different."

"Maybe so." He still acted perplexed, but she didn't pursue it and decided to change the topic to get his mind on something else. "So, have you heard how much longer you'll be locked in this place?"

"My doctor hasn't said. How about you?"

"The antibiotic is working fine—no fever for days. I'll get another X ray tomorrow."

"So you may be leaving sooner than me."

"I've been here for over a week and I'd like to leave. Wouldn't you?"

"Sure." But his tone was hesitant. "It's a little scary, though, thinking of going outside these walls when I still can't see."

"Will someone be with you when you go home?"

He shook his head. "Both my folks work, so I'll have to be on my own for most of the day. It wouldn't be so bad if I could see. I'm behind in all my schoolwork and I'm in accelerated classes. I'll probably never catch up."

"Are we having a pity party?"

"You're not going to let me feel sorry for myself? Not even just a little?"

"It won't help." Carley toyed with her fork. She wasn't being insensitive to his plight, but she knew how senseless it was to sit around complaining about what couldn't be changed. Life went on whether a person participated in it or not. "But I know how it feels to be swamped with schoolwork. That's enough to give anybody a downer."

He laughed. "Well, I'm not ready to learn braille and I don't want to spent the summer in school, so I'm not sure how I'll catch up."

"Why don't you have Steve or Jason tape your class lectures for you? Maybe then you wouldn't fall so far behind."

He straightened in the chair. "Why didn't I think of that?" He sounded amazed that something so obvious could have eluded him.

"You don't have a brain as devious as mine?" she offered playfully.

"Carley, that's a great idea. My dad could arrange to have all my classes taped and I can keep up that way. Why, I might even be able to take tests orally."

She tapped his hand. "I charge big bucks for advice, you know."

"I'll pay." They laughed together, but soon Kyle grew quiet, thoughtful. "Can I tell you something?"

She nodded, then realized that he couldn't see her. "Sure," she said for emphasis.

"I like you."

She felt her mouth go dry. "I like you too."

"Once we both go home, can I call you? Visit with you?"

So long as you're blind, she thought, but she said, "Oh gosh, once you get back to regular life, you'll forget all about me."

Kyle grabbed her hand and held it tightly. "Not so, Carley. I'll never forget you."

She felt a wave of fear. There was no way they could have a relationship once they were both out of the hospital. Sooner or later someone would see her and tell Kyle the truth. Certainly there would be no way she could ever persuade Janelle to impersonate her again. How could she put him off without hurting his feelings or telling him more than she ever wanted him to know? "Why don't we wait and see how things go once we blow this place?"

"You don't want me to keep in touch, do you?" He looked dejected.

"I didn't say that."

"But it's what you meant. Is it because I could be permanently blind? Is it because you don't want to be stuck with a guy who's blind?"

"No way," she started to protest.

Kyle interrupted. "Steve and Jason told me how pretty you are. I can't figure out why you don't have a boyfriend, unless you're so beautiful that you can pick anyone you want. If that's the case, I don't stand a chance."

In her heart she longed to tell him that he was handsome, smart, nice—the most wonderful guy she'd ever known. And that having him for a boyfriend would be the greatest thing that ever happened to her. But of course she couldn't. She could never let him know how she truly felt. "I think we should not talk about this stuff," she said quietly. "I think we should have fun right now and not talk about tomorrow."

"But—"

"Please," she begged. "Let's just be friends as long as we're here."

"If that's what you want. . . ." He tried to keep the hurt out of his voice.

"It's what I want."

Eleven

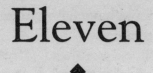

"You're going home? Lucky you." Reba gave Carley a wistful look. "I sure am going to miss you."

"I'll call you," Carley said, feeling sorry for Reba, who was still recovering from her abdominal surgery. "And before you know it, you'll be headed home too." Home for Reba was a small town in middle Tennessee, at least four hours from Knoxville and the hospital.

"When are you leaving?"

"My mom's packing my stuff and filling out the paperwork right now."

"I'm glad you stopped by to tell me. Have you told Kyle?"

Carley shook her head. "He's my next stop." She didn't let on how much she was dreading it.

"What have you decided to do about him?"

"Nothing. I figure that once he goes home, he'll get on with his life."

Reba dismissed the idea with a wave of her hand. "I think you're dreaming. I think he's going to want to see you."

"Don't say that. You and I both know it's impossible."

"Wrong. You *think* it's impossible, so you won't change your mind about telling him the truth."

Carley squealed, "Will you stop it already! I know what I'm doing."

Reba shook her head in exasperation. "Never mind. It's like talking to a brick wall." She grinned. "Anyway, keep your promise and call me. I know we haven't been friends for long, but you're my best friend ever and I want things to work out for you. You know, Carley, in spite of the way your face looks, you really do have a shot at being normal."

"Just how do you figure that?"

Reba's gaze led to the wheelchair parked near her bed. "I wish my face was the only thing messed up about me."

Impulsively Carley leaned down and hugged her. "I'll be in touch." She positioned her crutches under her arms and retreated from the room.

She stopped at Kyle's door, took a deep breath, and knocked. When he called, "Come in," she did.

"I got my walking papers," she told him without preamble.

His bandages couldn't hide his disappointment. "I'll miss you."

"That's what Reba said. Maybe I should start a fan club. Charge a fee." Carley kept her voice light and breezy.

"You said you'd be back for PT. Will you come up and visit with me?" he asked.

"You bet. I'll even bring you some new Books on Tape."

He held out his hand and she reached out and grasped it. His grip felt warm and strong and she wished she didn't ever have to let go. "You take care of yourself," he said.

"You too."

"You did mean what you said the other night about staying friends, didn't you?"

"I meant it." She was telling him what he wanted to hear and only hoped he wouldn't hate her when he figured out the truth—that she had no intention of ever seeing him again.

Without warning, Kyle reached up and caught the side of her face with his hand. She gasped, but then realized he was cupping the right side, the normal side. "Don't be mad," he said softly. "I've wanted to touch you for the longest time."

Just so long as his fingers didn't venture to the left side of her face, she didn't mind. "It's all right," she said, glad she had crutches for support because her knees had gone weak with anxiety and emotion.

He smoothed his thumb along her cheek, brushing the fringe of her eyelashes and the bridge of her nose. *Too close!* her mind warned. Carley pulled back. "Please don't," he whispered. "Can I touch your hair?"

She gulped. "Okay."

His fingers moved upward until they stroked the tips of her thick, dark hair. He wound strands around his hand, tugging them gently, tenderly. He rolled long clusters between his thumb and fingers, as if testing the texture. As if tasting it with his sense of touch. He reached higher, combed his fingers through the thickness, and said, "Very soft. I figured it would be."

Her breath caught in her throat and she could scarcely breathe. Tears stung her eyes. She longed to have him kiss her. If only . . . *if only*.

He withdrew his hand and brought his fingers to his nose and sniffed deeply. "Smells like flowers. And sunshine." He turned his face toward her, and she touched the corners of the bandages on his eyes. They were the barrier that held him prisoner, yet protected her. "I've noticed that scent every time you've come into my room. I've wondered if it was your hair or some perfume."

"New shampoo. The ad campaign said it would drive guys wild," she joked, hoping to make him laugh and break the tension.

He smiled. "Funny girl. But you don't always have to make a joke."

Humor was the only way she knew of dealing with intense emotional moments. "I've got to go." She stepped backward.

"I'll be seeing you, pretty Carley."

She winced because his words had stung. "Goodbye, Kyle."

She hurried next door, where her mother looked up from the suitcase she was packing. "There you are. I wondered where you ran off to." She paused and eyed Carley narrowly. "Are you all right? You look like you're crying."

"I'm fine, Mom. I was just saying goodbye."

Her mother shook her head, bemused. "You never cease to amaze me. You've always said you hated hospitals, and now you're crying because you have to leave this one. I'd have thought you'd never wanted to see the inside of this place again."

"I don't, Mom. Call the nurse and tell her

I'm ready for the wheelchair ride downstairs." She turned to the mirror and stared at the twisted half of her face, then jerked her hair back into a ponytail. Suddenly she didn't want anything to obstruct her true image, her real self. She didn't want to forget that what Kyle had made her feel was an illusion. She would never be normal. Or pretty. She mustn't ever forget. *Never!*

At home Carley moped around the house for the rest of the afternoon, unable to shake a case of the blues. She missed the routine of the hospital. Most of all, she missed Kyle. The next morning Janelle asked, "You want a ride to school? Jon's picking me up."

"I'll catch the bus," Carley said. "The sooner I get back into my regular routine, the better."

"Mom wants me to take you to PT tomorrow afternoon. Trouble is I have ensemble practice every day after school. State competition is in March, and if we don't practice every day, we'll never get a superior rating."

"I can drive myself."

"Tell that to Mom."

"I'm telling you, I can drive. There's nothing wrong with my right foot, and that's the one that controls the car."

"You'll have to clear it with Mom," Janelle said.

"How will you get home if I persuade her?"

"Jon will bring me."

"I forgot about lover boy."

"Be nice. I'll give up ensemble practice on the days you have PT if Mom says you can't drive yourself."

"You shouldn't have to do that."

Janelle shrugged. "I hate practice."

But Carley could tell that her sister really did want to practice. It was her senior year and her final opportunity to earn a superior rating at state chorus competitions. "Let me talk to Mom."

At school she felt as she always did—a nonparticipant, on the outside looking in. Her classes weren't a struggle; schoolwork came easily to her. But blending into the social scenery was something else again. A few kids spoke to her, asked her how her leg was doing, but most looked past her. Or over her. Or through her as if she hardly existed. She couldn't wait for the bell to ring, marking the end of the day, so that she could go home and forget all about high school and how she didn't fit in.

She told herself that in a few days she'd toughen up and it wouldn't matter. But the truth was that someone—Kyle—had treated her as if she were pretty and desirable. Now she had to return to being the ugly duckling, and it was difficult.

She was deep in thought, fiddling with the combination lock on her locker after school, balancing books and crutches, knowing she had to hurry if she was going to make it to her bus stop, when her notebook slipped from her hands and spilled on the hall floor.

Kids pouring out of rooms scurried past, stepping all over the binder. She could only watch helplessly, for she was unable to stoop down and rescue her notebook for fear of being trampled. All at once a boy's voice said, "Let me get that for you, babe."

She spun, forgetting to shield her face. Her rescuer was tall with dark hair and brown eyes. He was smiling, but as he caught sight of her face, his smile faded, and shocked surprise took its place. "I'll get it," she snapped, and struggled to hold her crutches with one hand while she bent over.

Then another male voice intervened. "Problems, Carley?"

It was Jon. He stooped and gathered up her notebook and scattered papers. He stood and glared at the other boy, still standing, staring. Jon snarled, "What's your problem? If you're not going to help, get out of the way."

The boy darted off.

"Dumb jerk," Jon muttered under his breath.

Carley straightened, her body burning with humiliation. "Thanks for retrieving my stuff," she said, grabbing for the notebook.

Jon held it back. "Wait."

"I've got to hurry or I'll miss my bus." She couldn't bear to look him in the eye. Couldn't stand knowing that he'd seen her humiliated by a stranger's look.

"I'm hanging around waiting for Janelle. Will you wait with me?" Jon asked.

"I can't."

Jon reached out and took her arm. "I want to talk to you, Carley. There're some things I need to say. Some things I *have* to say. You can get a ride home with Janelle and me, so don't run off. Hear me out. Please."

Twelve

The second bell rang and Carley sighed. "Well, I don't have much choice, do I? I'll never make it in time to catch my bus now."

Jon took her books and stacked them atop his. "Come on," he urged.

"Where to?"

"To the atrium."

The high school was built in the shape of a wheel, with the atrium at its hub and halls poking outward like spokes. With benches, potted plants, and a large overhead skylight, the atrium became an indoor student gathering place between classes and before and after school hours. Once there, Carley settled on a concrete bench emblazoned with the school seal. Jon sat down beside her and gestured toward the Fine Arts hallway. "Janelle has to come this way, so she'll see us."

Carley looked at her watch. Janelle wouldn't be out of practice for another forty-five minutes. She didn't think she and Jon could fill up the time simply talking, but she had no choice. "All right," she said, folding her hands in her lap, "What do you want to say to me? Ask suggestions for a Valentine's Day gift for my sister?"

"Buying Janelle presents isn't ever a problem."

Carley hadn't figured it would be. Pretty girls like Janelle always got gifts for Valentine's Day. "So then what can lowly little me do for you?"

"First off, I'm really crazy about Janelle."

"So tell me something I don't know."

"I also know you don't like me very much and I want to tell you that I don't blame you. I've acted like a real jerk."

Amazed by his confession, Carley stared at him. "Well, we do agree on some things."

In spite of her put-down, Jon smiled. "You do have a way of delivering a line, Carley."

"Don't you know? Comedy is my forte."

He rubbed the palms of his hands over the fabric of his jeans, and she could tell that he was nervous. "I know that you could have ruined things between Janelle and me if you wanted to."

"Why would I do that?"

"Some girls might have done it. If . . . if they overheard their sister's boyfriend saying rude stuff he didn't mean."

Carley shrugged, remembering the day in the gym when she'd heard him call her a dog. "It's ancient history, Jon. No use dredging it up."

"It was dumb of me. I didn't know you were there that day, and I was smarting off for the guys, acting like a big shot. I'm really sorry because I know it hurt you."

He looked miserable, and she almost felt sorry for him. "I've heard worse," she said. "When a person doesn't look normal, she hears a lot worse."

"I haven't been able to forget it," he said.

"Especially now that I know you better. And now that I know how much Janelle cares about you."

"She does?" Carley was mildly surprised. She'd always thought of Janelle as somewhat self-centered and too focused on her own life to have much interest in Carley's.

"She's like a bulldog sometimes. Nobody dares say anything mean about you, 'cause if she hears about it, she marches right up to them and makes them apologize. She tells them what a hero you are to have survived cancer and show up in school every day in spite of the way the doctors left your face. I heard her go off on someone once, and after five minutes of talking about how brave and special you are, she had the girl in tears."

Carley couldn't have been more shocked if he'd told her Janelle had sprouted a second head. "Janelle? My sister?"

"Don't you know how much she protects you?"

At a loss for words, Carley shook her head.

"Well, she does. She's changed my viewpoint about people who are handicapped. Or at least, people who aren't normal. And after getting to know you better, I agree with her. You're all right, Carley. You kept my secret when you could have ruined things between me and Janelle."

She blinked, and turned her head, overwhelmed by both his apology and his revelation about her sister's fierce loyalty toward her. "I wouldn't try to break up the two of you."

"You know that thing she did for you at the hospital with the guy next door—pretending to be you—was hard on her."

"I know she hated to lie for me."

"It was more than that," Jon said. "She told me later that sitting in that wheelchair gave her a new perspective on the world. She told me that she thinks it should be mandatory for every healthy teenager in the country to go around in a wheelchair for one day so that they can see what life's like for people who are maimed or deformed. She said that the world looks different when you're eye level with a person's waist and helpless."

Carley saw admiration stamped all over

his face and realized that she'd been as guilty of prejudice toward Janelle as others often were of *her*. How had she been so oblivious of her own sister's thoughts and feelings? "I'm glad you told me," Carley said. "I *think* I am . . . geez, now I'll have to really be nice to her."

Jon grinned and stood up. "I've never felt about any girl the way I feel about Janelle. I mean, she's pretty and all, but she's also special in other ways."

"You're a real cheerleader, Jon."

His face reddened. "Look, I didn't mean to go on and on. And I'd appreciate it if you didn't go telling her that I turned into a slobbering puppy over her."

"Well, as one dog to another, I think I can keep your secret," Carley said with a straight face.

Jon looked startled. "I told you I was sorry about saying that."

"I'm kidding," she said with a smile. "Lighten up."

He grinned sheepishly. "Thanks for understanding."

"Your secret's safe with me."

Just then Janelle came sauntering up the hallway, books balanced on her hip. "Hi, you two." She glanced from one to the other. "Boy, you look deep in conversation. Am I interrupting anything? What's up?"

"Nothing," Carley and Jon said in unison.

Janelle eyed them suspiciously. "It doesn't look like nothing."

"You're out early," Carley said, switching gears.

"Only fifteen minutes. I thought you were taking the school bus home."

"I changed my mind."

"I asked her to ride with us," Jon explained.

"So, let's get home." Carley stood and retrieved her crutches. "I have homework to do."

"I've got your books," Jon said. "I'll carry them to the car."

Quickly he and Carley took off side by side, leaving a befuddled Janelle to tag along behind.

It wasn't until the next afternoon when Janelle was driving Carley to her PT appointment that Janelle brought up the incident again. Their mother had categorically refused to allow Carley to drive herself. At least not until she was farther along in her therapy.

Janelle said, "When I came up yesterday, the two of you were totally engrossed in conversation. And when I said hello, you both acted as if I'd intruded on some clandestine meeting."

"You want to talk about this now?"

"Why not? I think the two of you were up to something and it involved me."

Carley felt her cheeks color. "Not true. We were just talking."

"Let's not argue. Just tell me what you and Jon were talking about."

Carley thought fast. "Um—Valentine's Day. He was asking my opinion on what to get you."

"I know you don't care for Jon." Janelle ignored the whole Valentine's Day story.

"He's all right."

"You said that before, but you didn't mean it."

"I've changed my opinion."

"Why?"

Carley sighed, and fiddled with the buttons on the radio. "I've gotten to know him and there's more to him than I once thought."

"Such as." Janelle repositioned the car's rearview mirror.

"He's not a total loser."

"Thanks for the endorsement."

"I didn't mean it that way. I wasn't sure Jon liked me. It seemed as if he was always avoiding me, and I figured it was because he couldn't deal with my looks."

"Jon's not that way." Janelle defended him.

"I know that now. I'm just not around guys very much, so sometimes I don't know what to say. Or how to act."

"You do all right with Kyle."

"You know he's different."

"Are you going to visit him today after your PT appointment?"

Carley stared out the window. The Tennessee countryside looked brown and stark, making her realize what a long, dreary month January could be. "I'm not sure I should."

"Why not?"

"Why prolong the agony? Once I left the hospital, I made up my mind to forget about him."

Janelle pulled into the parking lot adjacent to the physical therapy building attached to the Knoxville hospital. She put the car into park and turned off the engine. "I think you're making a mistake," she said quietly.

"How could it be a mistake to keep some guy who thinks I'm beautiful from learning the truth?" Carley leaned her head against the seat headrest and looked up through the windshield into the blustery gray sky. Without the engine to keep the heater going, the car's interior was chilling fast.

"Because you've got a rotten perception of physical beauty and its importance," Janelle said. "Because, believe me, being pretty isn't all it's cracked up to be. In fact sometimes it's the most awful burden in the world."

Thirteen

"I find that really hard to believe," Carley said after a few minutes had passed in silence. "How can being pretty be a handicap?"

"Because when a person's pretty, that's all people expect her to be. She isn't appreciated for anything except her physical appearance."

"What's so horrible about that?" Carley wanted to know. "I think it would be nice to have somebody look at me and say, 'She's pretty,' instead of 'Look, a freak.'"

"Anybody who puts a value on another person just because of his or her physical attractiveness is pitiful." Janelle's hazel eyes fairly crackled with conviction. "I don't want people hanging around with me because I look good, but because they *like* me."

"Get a grip," Carley insisted. "That's just not the way things are in the real world. All my life I've heard kids make fun of other kids because they were different—even before this happened to my face. I remember in the fifth grade there was this fat girl in my class. She wore thick glasses, too, and everybody made fun of her. Sometimes to the point of making her cry."

Carley dropped her gaze as she spoke, recalling the girl with clarity. "I'm sorry to say I teased her too. In fact after my surgery I wondered if leaving me deformed was God's way of paying me back for being mean to her."

Janelle recoiled. "You can't believe that! God's not that way. What about all the others who teased her? Did they get cancer and get left scarred?"

"Not that I know of." Carley stared hard at her hands as if they might hold some answer. "But why did this happen to me? Why did I have to get left with half a face?"

Janelle reached over and squeezed Carley's

shoulder. "Nobody has that answer. And trying to come up with one could drive you nuts."

"As if I'm not already."

Janelle wagged her finger. "Only when it comes to guys."

"And guys are the worst. You wouldn't know because you've always had to beat them off with a stick, but they only go after girls who are pretty. Cripes, you've had a zillion boyfriends."

"A zillion?" Janelle rolled her eyes. "I've dated a few, but most of them hardly see me as a person, just someone they can show off to their friends."

Carley wasn't the least bit sympathetic. She said, "I'm sixteen years old and I've never had a date." Old hurts welled up inside her. "Why do you suppose that is? Could it be because I'm not pretty? Why isn't my wonderful personality taken into consideration?"

"Now you're being sarcastic."

"No. I'm being realistic. I'm never going to have a date. No guy's ever going to ask me out or take me anywhere out in public."

Janelle sighed heavily. "I know it seems that way now."

"You bet it does."

"Kyle might just be the one if you'd give him half a chance."

"So long as he's blind and so long as we don't have to mingle with the rest of the world, Kyle and I can have a thing for each other. But the minute his vision clears, or his friends meet the real Carley, it'll be over between us. Trust me. I know what I'm talking about."

Janelle balled her fist and pounded the steering wheel. "You are *so* stubborn and bullheaded."

Carley quickly brought her fingers up to either side of her head like horns and snorted.

Janelle shook her head while trying to suppress a smile. "I give up. But someday you'll find out I'm right. Looks aren't nearly as important as you think they are." Janelle pointed toward the hospital. "Go on and keep your PT appointment before we have to fight about this."

Carley grasped the car door handle. "What are you going to do? It's too cold to sit out here in the car."

"I'm going into the hospital cafeteria and have a cup of hot chocolate." She reached into the backseat and grabbed a book. "And study for an American History test." She made a face.

"I'll come there after I finish."

As Carley was fishing out her crutches, Janelle asked, "So what did you tell Jon?"

"About what?"

"About what to buy me for Valentine's Day."

Now it was Carley who grinned. "I told him to think gold and pricey."

Janelle returned a smile and nodded. "Good advice, little sister."

Together they walked to the Rehabilitation building, where Janelle took the covered walkway to the hospital and Carley went inside the PT center. When she'd completed her therapy, she ventured over to the hospital, but not to the cafeteria. Instead, she took the elevator up to her former floor, and, with heart thudding, she ambled down the hall to Kyle's room. The door was ajar and she halted in the doorway.

In the room she saw Kyle down on all fours, methodically feeling the floor in a circular pattern. Fascinated, she watched, realizing he was searching for something. Under the bed she spied the small foam rubber baffle that fit over the end of an earplug for comfort when wearing a headset, and she knew that's what he was trying to find. She wanted to shout, "I see it!" She wanted to rush in and pick it up for him. Yet she did nothing but watch him pat the floor and grunt in frustration.

Pity for him flooded through her. If he didn't regain his sight, he would spend the remainder of his life learning to adjust to living blind in a seeing world. If he remained sightless, he'd never get to realize his dreams of working for NASA or of flying an airplane.

Feelings of guilt twisted her insides like a sharp knife. To protect his illusions of her, she'd wanted him never to be able to see her. How unfair! No one deserved to be confined to a world of darkness if it was preventable or correctable. Just because she was limited to a less than normal life was no reason to selfishly wish the same sentence on him. Silently she pleaded to be forgiven for her attitude. *Let Kyle get his sight back*, she begged with all her heart.

All at once Kyle reared up and sat stockstill. "Who's there?" he asked.

Caught off guard, Carley pressed her back to the door frame. She should speak up. But she didn't.

"Hey, I know somebody's in the room with me. Tell me who."

Still she kept quiet.

"You're being rude, you know. I can't see you, but I know you're there. Why don't you say something?" His brow furrowed and his voice sounded angry.

Why don't I say something? Carley couldn't believe she was behaving this way. Couldn't understand why she was provoking him. But her vocal cords refused to respond. It was as if they'd been cut; she was helpless to reveal herself.

"Talk to me!" Kyle shouted.

She backed out of the room, desperate to be gone. One crutch caught on a corner of the door and she almost went sprawling, but she managed to regain her balance without making any noise. She spun and barreled down the hall toward the elevator. Tears almost blinded her, and her breath came in rapid gasps, half sobs.

Behind her she could hear Kyle calling, "Whoever you are, you're a stinking coward! You have no right to sneak up on a blind person, then run away. Do you hear me?"

Carley jabbed frantically at the elevator button, terrified that a nurse would hear Kyle and discover her trying to escape. The elevator came and she flung herself through the opening doors. Mercifully it was empty and she sagged against the side, heaving great breaths of air. Her hands shook and her knees wobbled, but she'd escaped without him knowing who'd been in his room.

She finger-combed her hair and tried to regain her composure during the ride to ground level, where Janelle was waiting in the cafeteria. "You must be seriously deranged," she told herself shakily under her breath. Kyle was right, only a coward would have refused to face him. Why hadn't she greeted him? Stayed for a visit? Why had she gone up in the first place when she'd told Janelle she wasn't going to? When she had sworn to herself she would never see him again?

"You're horrible, Carley Mattea," she muttered to herself. *You upset Kyle and ran off. You were mean and hateful.*

Janelle called out to her, gathered up her book, and hurried over. "What took you so long? Hey, are you okay?" She squinted at Carley. "You look discombobulated." The expression was a longtime favorite of their Southern grandmother.

"I'm all right." She clenched her hands hard around the grips of her crutches. "Tell me, what does 'combobulated' look like?"

Janelle ignored Carley's attempt to divert the conversation. "Did your physical therapy hurt?" Automatic sympathy flooded her pretty features.

"A little," she lied.

"They overworked your leg, didn't they?"

"As Jon says, 'no pain, no gain.' "

"Well, I'm glad I'm driving so that you can relax."

Carley didn't want to relax; she wanted to forget she'd ever met Kyle Westin and experienced what it was like to be thought pretty and normal. Whoever said "ignorance is bliss" was correct. Before, she could only speculate what it would be like. Now that she knew, she hated it. The feeling was painful and sad. Like a taste of some wonderful fruit that a person could savor only once and then never forget.

In the car she reclined the seat and closed her eyes, hoping that Janelle would get the message that she didn't want to talk. Because there was no way she could ever explain that it wasn't her leg that hurt. It was her heart.

Fourteen

Two days later Carley still hadn't figured out why she'd behaved so foolishly at the hospital. Deciding that she had to get it off her mind, she called the hospital, dialed Kyle's extension, and heard the voice of a stranger. Kyle had checked out and returned home. She hung up, glad he'd been released, but disappointed that she hadn't been able to talk to him.

She told herself it was for the best. No contact was the best thing. Now she could get on with her life, and he could get on with his.

Her mother took off from the bookstore to drive Carley to her appointment with her orthopedist, Dr. Olson. "If he says it's all right for me to drive, will you let me?" Carley asked.

"If he agrees, yes," her mother answered.

Dr. Olson had his technician take X rays of Carley's leg, and once the film was developed, he put the various views up on a light-board and studied them while Carley and her mom looked on. "Your bone looks good. The pins are holding fine and the infection is entirely cleared up. I know you didn't want to be in the hospital for ten days, but it was the best course of treatment for you. The IV antibiotic really did the job."

There was no way to tell him just how much of an impact the hospitalization had had on her life, so Carley simply asked, "How much longer will I have to wear this thing?"

He looked at her chart. "Let's see—surgery was three weeks ago, at the beginning of January. It takes six to eight weeks for a bone to knit, so maybe as early as mid-February."

"She would have been out of the cast sooner if it hadn't been for the infection,"

Carley's mother observed, making it sound as if the doctor was somehow at fault.

"Osteomyelitis isn't common, but it can happen." Dr. Olson said good-naturedly. "The important thing is that Carley's well on the road to recovery now."

"Time flies when you're having fun," Carley interjected. She saw no reason for her mother to blame the doctor for something that was nobody's fault.

"And what about her tendons? You told us that she may have to have further surgery on them."

"Let's see how she does with PT once the cast is off. Maybe further surgery is avoidable. In the meantime if you want to hang up your crutches, you can."

"I can manage without them," Carley said.

"But," her mother said doggedly, "her infection had nothing whatsoever to do with the fact that she once had cancer, does it?"

"Absolutely nothing," Dr. Olson assured her. "The infection could have happened to anyone."

Carley saw her mother look relieved, and until then she hadn't realized the cancer issue had been weighing on her mind. It certainly hadn't weighed on hers. Later, when they were driving home, Carley said, "Mom, my cancer was four years ago, and the oncologist only sees me once a year. He told you I was cured. If the doctors aren't worried about it, why are you?"

"I'm not worried," her mother contended. "I believe you're cured. I just don't want us to be blindsided like that again. I mean, who expected headaches to turn into a cancerous tumor?"

"And who expected the 'fix' to leave my face like this?" Carley finished quietly.

"It was the only way to save your life." Her mother glanced over at her. "We never talk about it. You seem so well adjusted and all. You crack jokes. You forge ahead with life. And when I look at you, I don't see it anymore."

"How could you *not* see it? My face is deformed!"

"Not to me. To me I see my beautiful little daughter who's alive."

Carley sighed. "Well, the rest of the world sees a girl with a messed-up face."

"Do you tell people what happened? Do you let them know how you got this way?"

"Oh, sure, Mom, right! Just what I want to do—deliver my life story to everyone who stares at me."

Her mother fiddled with the heater controls, partly out of being flustered, Carley figured, because the car was plenty warm. "Well, people like that are insensitive and callow. People can't help the way they look, just the way they act."

Her mother's view of the world seemed simplistic to Carley. And naive. But perhaps a person needed to live with something before she understood it. "I've made up my mind that everybody would be better off if people wore paper bags over their heads. You know, with little cutouts for eyes and mouths. That way we'd all be on equal footing when it comes to a social life."

Her mom smiled. "It seems you've been giving everything a whole lot more thought these days. Don't think I haven't noticed the way you've moped around the house ever since you came home from the hospital. Care to tell me why?"

"No reason," she said, turning to gaze out the window. She couldn't tell her mother about Kyle and the emotions he'd stirred up in her. Emotions that might have never surfaced if he could have seen her face. She caught sight of her face in the side mirror and purposefully turned so that she didn't have to look at her own reflection.

"Maybe I've forgotten how traumatic high school can be," her mother mused, half aloud, watching Carley from the corner of her eye. "I think it's time we started making the rounds to plastic surgeons again."

Carley shrugged listlessly. "We did that, remember? They told us there was nothing they could do to fix me."

"But things change in medicine every day. There are new technologies, new break-throughs. They do things now they couldn't do a few years ago. I think we should check it out again."

"Do you think they can make me look normal?"

"I think we should go ask. Do you want

me to set up an appointment? Do you want to think about it for a while?"

Carley didn't have to think about it. She wanted it more than anything. She wasn't being unrealistic; she knew she might never be pretty no matter what they did to her face. But she had to look better than this. Otherwise, what kind of future did she have other than joining the circus as a sideshow exhibit?

"Sure, Mom. Let's do it. Let's see if all the smart doctors can put Carley together again."

On Saturday Carley went to work in the bookstore, her first day of work since before her accident. She arrived with Janelle before the start of the business day, and while her sister set up the register and readied the counter area for customers, Carley walked along the aisles, inspecting the shelves.

"Boy, Mom sure has the place junked up," she said over her shoulder.

"She's a sucker for Cupid," Janelle said. "Every time a publisher offers a new display, she makes room for it."

Carley leaned over to examine one lavish cardboard unit colored with vivid red hearts, nosegays of violets, and embossed ribbons of white Victorian lace. She stuck out her tongue.

"That's not nice," Janelle said, coming up beside her.

Carley blushed, but pretended she wasn't embarrassed about her childish antics. "Sorry, but I think Valentine's Day is a waste."

"Hush. You'll hurt Cupid's feelings."

"Let the little dirtbag suffer."

Janelle giggled. "Does this mean you're not going to send anybody special a card?"

"Who would I send a card to?"

Janelle crossed her arms and tapped her toe and waited patiently for Carley to figure it out.

"Kyle?" Carley squealed. "Are you implying I should send one to Kyle?"

"And why not?"

"He's blind. He couldn't see it anyway."

"That's rude, Carley."

Instantly she felt ashamed. "I . . . um . . . just don't think I should send him one. It's a dumb thing for a girl to do. Guys are supposed to send cards, not girls."

"What rock did you crawl out from under? If you like somebody, you should let him know. What could it hurt to send the guy a little Valentine? It might even make him feel good."

Carley started to list all the reasons why not, when the phone rang. Janelle hurried to the front desk and answered it. She cupped her hand over the mouthpiece and held it out to Carley. "It's for you."

"Me? No one ever calls me here. Who is it?"

"Your personal Cupid."

"Kyle?" Carley felt her mouth go dry. "Tell him I'm busy. Tell him I'm not working today." Her heart began to thud with panic.

"She's on her way to the phone," Janelle said sweetly into the receiver. "Give her a minute to get here."

Carley shot her a threatening look, but she came forward and took the receiver. She pretended it was Janelle's neck and squeezed it extra hard.

"I'll be in the back," Janelle said, breezing away.

Carley took a deep breath and said hello.

"Hello yourself. Remember me? Your friendly next-door hospital neighbor?"

"Of course. How goes it?"

"I thought you were going to call me."

"I did, but you'd checked out."

He was quiet for a moment. "I left my phone number with the nurses. In case you asked."

"I—I didn't think of asking."

"I asked them for yours, but they said it was against hospital policy to give out the information. Then I remembered about your parents' bookstore."

"So, here I am." She forced herself to sound perky.

"I was going to call you last week, but I wanted to wait until after my checkup on Friday."

Her heart hammered harder and she half dreaded, half hoped for what she knew he was about to tell her. "How did it go?"

"I can see, Carley. I'm going to be all right."

Fifteen

"That's wonderful, Kyle." Carley tried to control the tremor in her voice.

"Oh, my vision's not perfect. I've still got a long way to go."

"What do you mean?"

"Well, I'm real sensitive to light. But when he took my bandages off, I could see shapes. Everything was really blurry and my eyes watered like crazy, but things are looking clearer and sharper every day."

"So no more gauze pads?"

"I've graduated. I have to wear dark glasses if I go outside. Or even if I'm inside and the lights are bright. And my doctor still wants me to keep my left eye covered with a black patch for a while, but for the most part I can see again."

Carley twirled the phone cord around her finger. She knew she should keep asking him questions and be happy for him, but both were difficult for her to do when she had so much at stake in his answers. "How long before you're one hundred percent?"

"It may be weeks yet. And they still don't know if my vision will ever be twenty-twenty or not. I just wish I could lose this stupid eye patch. I look and feel ridiculous."

"Like a pirate, huh?"

"Worse. People come up to me all the time and ask me about it. Seems kind of rude to me, but still they ask."

She understood completely. "People are nosy. You have to ignore them."

He gave a short laugh. " 'Course my friends Steve and Jason tell me to consider the plus side."

"Such as?"

"It's a cool way to meet girls."

"Whatever works."

"But I told them I've already met the perfect girl."

Her hand had grown clammy on the receiver and she was having trouble keeping it tight on the slippery plastic. "That's nice of you to say."

"That's why I want to get together with you."

"Well I—"

"Not right yet," he added hastily. "I'd like my eyesight to clear up a little more so that I can see you. I'd like to ditch the patch too. I mean, when you can only see out of one eye, there's no depth perception. Uncool. I can't judge how close or how far away something is, which makes me fumble around a lot. But it sure beats not seeing at all."

"I'd guess so."

"Anyway, I want to meet you. See you with my own eyes. Steve and Jason are still talking about you."

She couldn't think of anything to say, but she was desperate to keep a meeting from happening.

"Listen to me," Kyle said apologetically. "I'm going on and on about me and I haven't once asked how you're doing. How's the leg?"

"I've ditched the crutches. And my doctor says I might be able to shed the cast by the middle of next month."

"Maybe in time for Valentine's Day?"

Carley's eyes darted to the calendar posted on the wall behind the desk. Sure enough, February fourteenth was pretty much in the middle of the next month. "Maybe."

"Well, whether you're in a cast or not, I'd like you to go to our school's spring dance with me. It's on the weekend after Valentine's Day."

"I don't dance."

"I don't either, but so what? We'll just go together, sit, and watch the others. It's being held at the big Marriott downtown; there'll be a banquet and everything. It's going to be really nice. Of course, I can't drive because of my eyes, but we'll go with Jason and Steve."

"I won't know anybody."

"You'll know me. Plus, you've met Jason and Steve. Their girlfriends are pretty nice. We'll all have a great time together."

Just then the door of the bookstore opened and a customer walked inside. "Uh

—can we talk about this later? Business is starting up and I have to go to work."

"You bet. But don't hang up without giving me your home phone number."

Quickly she told him, then said goodbye. Janelle came behind the counter as she was hanging up the phone. "Thanks a lot for making me take that call." Nervous perspiration caused Carley's bangs to stick to her forehead.

"I'm not going to lie for you. I did that once and I hated it." Janelle smiled at the customer who was browsing the stacks. "What did Kyle want?"

"He can see again and he wants to meet me. He wants to take me to some dance his school's having." Carley sagged into a chair behind the counter. "Not me of course. *You*."

"And who's fault is that?"

"I'm not in the mood for a lecture." She glanced around to see if the customer had his back to the front desk. She hated the idea of the man staring at her once he saw her face. "I'm going into the back room and start unboxing and cataloging."

"I wish you'd been honest with Kyle from the very beginning."

"Well, I wasn't, so start helping me figure out a way to keep this face-to-face meeting from ever happening."

Janelle threw up her hands and backed away. "Oh no, baby sister. You're on your own this time."

"Aw—come on."

Janelle ignored her plea. "I'm going to see if this man needs help." She swept from behind the counter and hurried over to the browsing customer.

Carley hauled herself to the backroom, where boxes of new books were stacked and waiting. She lowered herself onto a nearby chair and stared gloomily at the floor. Life wasn't fair! For the first time in her life, she'd been asked out on a date. And by the one boy she'd give anything to go out with. Except that she couldn't because the girl he thought was her, wasn't. And the girl he thought was pretty, was not.

She should have been honest with him from the start. Except that if she had been honest, he would never have wanted to see her in the first place. And the days that she'd known him in the hospital had been wonderful, because for just a short time she'd been treated as if she were a normal girl.

Carley sighed and told herself to get to work. Thinking about Kyle was only depressing her. She'd think of some reason to keep him from meeting her. After all, she'd been able to fool him and his friends once. She'd have to do it again. She'd have to come up with something that would end her relationship with Kyle once and for all. There was no choice. She'd shut the door on their friendship forever.

That night Carley did something that she hadn't done in years. She took the family photo album off the shelf and retreated to her room, closed the door, climbed onto her bed, and spread it out in front of her.

She started with her baby pictures. She turned the pages and saw herself transform from cute, chubby, and bald with a broad, toothless smile into a gangly seven-year-old with front teeth missing and lank dark hair in braids. By the time she was nine, the teeth were back and the hair was brushing her shoulders.

Her fifth-grade school picture was the last one ever taken with her face in one piece. Carley stared long and hard at the grinning photo. At the perfect symmetry of her nose and eyes. At the full, dimpled cheeks and the smooth, flawless complexion. At her forehead uncluttered by bangs. Why, by anybody's standards she had been cute, even pretty in a childlike, innocent way.

She ran her fingertips over the photograph, as if by touching it she might somehow absorb her former self into her present self. How wonderful it would be if she could align the two faces and superimpose the younger one onto her current one. How good it would be to fill in the sunken places of her "now" face with her "then" face.

She had been born whole and complete. At age twelve she'd been held hostage by cancer. And robbed of normalcy. No clever cosmetic makeover could ever make her look whole again. So, how did she mourn for this lost piece of herself? This missing part from the inside of her body that so affected the outside?

Carley sighed and shut the photo album. She caught sight of her reflection in the mirror over her dresser, but did not turn away. No need to ask, "Mirror, mirror on the wall, who's the fairest of them all?" Her mirror couldn't lie. The truth was stamped within its frame just as surely as it was stamped upon her face.

Now she resembled a piece of modern art—a painting by one of those artists who liked to paint people in the shapes of cubes and squares. Her face was right out of a futuristic drawing, lopsided and off-center. When she smiled, it caved in more tightly, like a flower turning in upon itself.

The phone call from Kyle had been wonderful and she was happy that he was able to see. But she was more determined than ever that he shouldn't ever see her. For the girl he'd created in his imagination was the girl she wanted him to think of as Carley. She still wasn't sure how she was going to get him out of her life once and for all, but she was determined to do so. No matter how much it tore her up to do it. No matter how badly it broke her heart.

Sixteen

"I'm ready to meet you, Carley. It's all I've been thinking about."

Kyle's words on the phone ten days later caused Carley's heart to skip a beat and her stomach to constrict. She'd taken the call in her room on the portable phone and lay across her bed, clutching it to her ear. Her leg in the cast felt as if it weighed a ton— almost as heavy as her heart felt in her chest. "I've been thinking about it too," she said.

"And the dance? Will you go with me?"

"I can't."

"Why not? I told you I don't care about dancing. I just want to be with you. I want to show you off."

"I'm not a prize cow, you know."

"That's not what I mean and you know it." His voice sounded hurt. "I miss you, Carley. I miss talking to you. Visiting with you. I even miss your Books on Tape. I have a bunch to return, you know."

"Just keep them. I can get more."

"What's wrong? Why don't you want to see me?"

Her heart was thudding so loudly that she was afraid he might hear it through the receiver. "I have something to tell you."

"Tell me. Please."

Her gaze fell on a photograph of Janelle and Jon taken over the Christmas holidays. They had their arms around each other and Jon was wearing a Santa hat. Inspiration flooded through her. "Remember in the hospital when you asked me if I had a boyfriend?"

"You said you didn't."

"Well, that wasn't exactly the truth."

"You have a boyfriend?"

"Yes. Jon and I've been going together for over a year, but we had a big fight before Christmas and sort of broke up."

"If you broke up—"

"But now we're back together," she added hastily.

"And the whole time you were in the hospital he never paid you a visit?"

"He was away on a skiing trip with his parents."

"At the start of the new semester?"

Carley chewed on her bottom lip. This wasn't going as well as she'd hoped. "What is this, Twenty Questions?" she asked. "Take my word for it, he and I had a fight but we've made up and we're together again."

"Why didn't you tell me this in the hospital?"

"I—I didn't know how."

"Simple. You say, 'Kyle, let me tell you about my boyfriend.' I remember asking you if you had one."

"Sorry. I didn't."

"And so you met my friends and let them think you liked me."

"I *do* like you." She began to squirm. "It's possible to like you *and* still have a boyfriend, you know. I really thought we had broken up for good when I met you in the hospital. But now that I'm back in school and all—well, I realized I still liked him." Lying to Kyle was difficult, but she felt she was in too deep to turn back now.

He didn't say anything for such a long time that she wondered if he'd put the phone aside and walked away. She asked, "Kyle?"

"I'm here."

"I—I'm sorry."

"I still want to meet you."

"What?" She couldn't believe he was being so insistent. "Why?"

"Carley, when I was in the hospital, you helped me more than anybody. The talks we had, the visits, the phone calls—all those things kept me from climbing the walls. I want to meet you. I want to see you for myself. I want to tell you thanks to your face."

"Jon's jealous," she blurted. "He doesn't like me seeing other guys."

"Couldn't he understand this one time? I'm not asking for much. After this one meeting I'll drop out of your life. I promise."

Her head was spinning, desperate to find a

way out of her dilemma. She didn't want him out of her life, but the need to protect herself was far more intense than her willingness to tell him everything. Suddenly an idea came to her. "Okay, all right, fair enough. I'll let you see me. But it has to be from a distance."

"How far? North Carolina?"

The sarcasm in his voice made her cringe. "I don't want Jon to know about you," she explained. "Please. If you care about me, you'll do me this favor."

Again there was a long pause. "All right. Whatever you want." She sagged with relief. "Where can I see you?" he asked.

She realized she had no place to tell him because she'd never been anyplace on a date. *Where would Jon take Janelle?* she wondered. She remembered her sister telling her about the Mudpie, a coffeehouse that had opened in September and had quickly gained favor with the older high school crowd. She asked Kyle if he'd heard of it.

"I've been there once. Before my accident."

"Well, that's where I'll be Friday afternoon with my boyfriend. That's when you can see me."

"What time?"

"Four-thirty."

"All right."

"But, Kyle, you can't come over and speak to me. You have to hang back. I—I wouldn't want Jon to know. He wouldn't like it."

"I won't embarrass you." His voice sounded emotionless. "Steve will be with me because he has to do the driving, but I'll make certain he keeps out of the way too."

"I—um-probably won't wave to you, or acknowledge you in any way." Carley nibbled on her bottom lip nervously.

"I understand the rules."

"I wish things could be different."

"You're the only one who can make things different."

She knew he was right. "I can't," she said softly into the phone. "I just *can't.*"

Carley cornered Jon in the atrium the next afternoon while he was waiting for Janelle to finish ensemble rehearsal. When she told him her plan, he balked. "Are you crazy? I can't do that."

"And why not? All I'm asking is that you take her to the Mudpie Friday afternoon and buy her coffee or a soda. I'll even pay for it."

Jon shook his head. "There isn't enough money. If she suspects anything, she'll kill me and disown you."

"Believe me, being disowned is preferable to your not helping me."

"Don't pressure me. I won't do it."

Tears of frustration welled up in her eyes. It wasn't easy for her to beg. "Kyle promised he'd keep out of the line of vision. He swore that all he'd do is look, then leave. You've got to help me, Jon. Please."

"Don't cry." He glanced nervously toward the hallway, where Janelle was soon to appear. "If Janelle sees you, she'll have to know why. Have you asked her if she'd do it for you?"

"She won't. I know she won't. And once she knows the plan, she'll never go to the Mudpie with you. No, it's better to take her, let Kyle slip in and see the two of you, and disappear. He'll see her, and Steve will tell him it's me, and he'll think I'm beautiful. Nobody will get hurt."

"Nobody?"

"All right—*I* won't get hurt. What's so terrible about that?"

Jon looked pained, indecisive. Carley felt as if he wanted to help, but was scared.

"This will be the end of it, Jon. Once Friday is over, the door will be closed and I'll never ask a favor of you again. Please help me."

On Friday Carley had a makeup test after school and missed the bus. That left her no choice but to accompany Jon and Janelle to the Mudpie, which worked out better because, with Carley along, even if Janelle happened to see Kyle and Steve in the coffee shop, she wouldn't be suspicious—Janelle knew Carley would never run the risk of bumping into Kyle. Her sister would never suspect that *she herself* had set up the meeting.

The three of them sat in a booth in the far back of the small coffee shop. Carley told them it would make her feel self-conscious if she sat anywhere else, and of course Janelle believed her. She fidgeted, watching the clock constantly. At exactly four-twenty she excused herself to go to the bathroom. There, in the small, protected hallway, Carley could peek around the corner without being seen.

The coffee shop was crowded with tables and booths filled with teens and groups of twenty-somethings preparing for weekend fun. A sofa, two easy chairs and a coffee table toward the front gave the place a homey atmosphere. Green plants hung on cords from the ceiling, and the aromas of exotic coffees and sweet-scented vanilla and cinnamon spiced the air. Carley would have enjoyed herself if she hadn't been so nervous.

When she saw Kyle come in the door, she caught her breath. He wore a wheat-colored cable-knit sweater, jeans, and dark glasses. Another boy was with him; she assumed it was Steve. Her heart wedged in her throat as she watched Kyle scan the room. She watched as Steve nudged him in the ribs. Kyle stared toward the booth where Jon sat with Janelle.

Janelle, oblivious to her surroundings,

leaned toward Jon, her face animated and smiling. Jon held her hand across the table, took a dollop of whipped cream from atop his cappuccino, and offered it to Janelle's pretty red mouth. Kyle watched the scene without expression. Knowing she was hurting him, Carley felt a terrible heaviness. She squeezed her eyes shut, and when she opened them again, Kyle and Steve were gone.

She gazed longingly at the space that had held him. At the sunlight playing through the glass window and leaving bright patches on the floor where he had stood. He was gone, just as he had promised. Her charade was over. She was safe, yet inside she felt no elation, no satisfaction. She felt hollow and empty.

Goodbye, Kyle. His dark glasses had hidden his eyes, and with a start she realized that she had never once looked into their depths. She didn't even know what color they were. And now she never would.

Seventeen

"Hello, Carley. I'm Dr. Chaffoo."

"Hi," she said, shaking the hand of the plastic surgeon. She took a seat beside her mother on the leather sofa in the doctor's plush office.

The doctor was good-looking, with a wide, generous smile, blue eyes, and brown hair flecked with gray. He didn't wear the white lab coat so typical of other doctors she had known, but instead was dressed in a well-tailored navy suit, crisp white shirt, and a colorful silk tie. Her mother had assured Carley that he had come highly recommended, and together they'd driven the thirty miles into Knoxville to meet with him about the possibility of reconstructing her face.

"I've obtained your medical charts and read through them," Dr. Chaffoo said, leafing through a thick manilla folder on his gleaming mahogany desk. "I've also talked to your oncologist and have a very thorough picture of what you went through four years ago."

"The question is," her mother interjected, "can you help my daughter? Can anything be done to give her a more normal appearance?"

"Is that what you want, Carley?"

"More than anything." Carley felt both anxious and excited. She was afraid to get her hopes up, yet she longed for him to tell her she was "fixable."

Dr. Chaffoo stood, came around his desk, raised her chin with his forefinger, and scrutinized her face. It made her feel self-conscious. She disliked anyone staring at her too intently. Gently he smoothed his thumb along the sunken contours of her cheek, eye, and nose, then returned to his chair. "In a

few minutes I'm going to take you into another room where I have an imaging computer and a camera set up. But first let's talk
about the realities of reconstructive surgery.
No matter how much plastic surgery you
have done, you'll always have a scar on your
face and some residual effects of your cancer
surgery. I can't make you perfect."

Carley felt her hopes sag. No one could
help her.

"However," the doctor continued, "I can
make you look a whole lot better."

"Tell us," her mother said.

"What plastic surgeons try to do with this
type of malformation is add symmetry back
to your face. As it is now, anyone who sees
you is automatically drawn to the defect because your face is out of proportion. If we fill
in the caved-in areas, your cheek can look
fuller, your eye can be elevated to align with
the other, and your nose can be recon-
structed to give you a more normal appearance."

Her mother asked, "But bone and tissue
were removed during her cancer surgery.

They told us it can't regrow. It's gone forever."

Carley looked straight at the doctor. "What do you use? Silly Putty? Paper and paste? Play-Doh?"

Dr. Chaffoo laughed heartily. "Good suggestions, but your body would reject such foreign substances. No . . . whenever possible I'd use your own body tissue, fat, and bone. Some silicone plastic if necessary."

"My tissue? How?"

"First I'll send you to a radiology lab and have a three-dimensional CAT scan made of your head. This type of X ray will help me see you on the inside before I operate. It will give me exact dimensions of your nasal and cranial areas and offer me a model to follow for rebuilding. An old photograph of you will also be used for comparison."

"Like *The Terminator*?" She remembered her photo as a twelve-year-old, and a movie she'd once seen about a robot made to look human.

He laughed again. "I'll be able to see the extent of the area needing work, and that will help me gauge the amount of material I'll need to harvest for your surgeries."

"How many surgeries?" her mother wanted to know.

"Probably three. Each one about six months apart with two to three hours in the operating room and one to two days in the hospital for recovery."

Carley's hopes dipped. She hadn't expected it to take so long. "But that could take over a year and a half. I'll be a senior by the time I look acceptable."

"But you're so young," the doctor said. "Over the course of a lifetime what's eighteen months?"

My entire life in high school, she thought, but didn't say it. A normal social life would still elude her. And being able to meet Kyle face-to-face was a dream gone up in smoke. Secretly she'd harbored the hope that fixing her face might take less time and therefore give her another opportunity to work something out with him.

"You said you could use tissue from my daughter's own body. Tell us about that part." Her mother didn't even sense Carley's disappointment, but pressed the doctor for more details.

"I can take cartilage from behind your ear to replace nasal cartilage." He tugged on his ear to demonstrate flexibility. "Your ear will be fine and look perfectly normal."

"But what about bone? Could you take some from my leg?" She held up the leg in the cast. "I'm sure there's plenty to go around."

"Actually I'd use a calvarial bone graft—that's bone taken from your skull and grafted into existing bone in your cheek to provide a floor for fat I'd take from your abdomen or buttocks. The fat will plump out the area."

She stared at him. "You're going to take a chunk out of my head?"

"The skull's thick. You won't miss the fragment I'll take." She remembered what it had been like to be bald from chemo. It had taken years to grow her hair long again. As if reading her mind, Dr. Chaffoo said, "Don't worry, I won't have to shave your head. I'll take bone from in back of your hairline. You can brush the rest of your hair over the area. I'll insert the bone through an incision in your gum line." He raised his lip and pointed to the area above his upper teeth. "And the bone to enhance your eye area can be inserted through an incision under your eyelash line." He ran his finger along the lower lashes of his left eye.

Carley thought the whole idea sounded bizarre and creepy, and it made her stomach feel queasy. She glanced at her mother, who didn't look especially pleased with his descriptions either. "Sounds like fun," Carley said drolly. She recalled how horrible she looked following her surgery for the removal of the cancerous tumor.

"The stitches are exceedingly fine. I do them with a microscope." The doctor stood. "Come with me, Carley. I want to show you something."

In another room he took color photos of her, front and side views, and sent the picture electronically into a nearby computer. Her image popped up on the screen and she grimaced. She thought she looked ugly.

"Well, Mom, if the FBI ever puts these on the walls of the post office, I'll sue," she quipped.

"Watch this," Dr. Chaffoo said.

Carley leaned over his shoulder and watched as he moved the computer's mouse on its pad. Every few seconds she heard it click and slowly watched her face transform on the computer screen. With wonder she saw her left eye shift upward and the space between her nose and eye socket fill in. She watched the bridge of her nose swell and smooth, until her nose looked straight and perfectly formed. She saw her cheek plump and fill in like a round, full apple.

Minutes later Dr. Chaffoo leaned back in his chair and said, "Well, there you are, Carley. This is how I can make you look."

Beside her she heard her mother's breath come out in small sobs. And seeing the transformed image, Carley could scarcely catch her own breath. "I—I look all right. I look like a regular girl," she whispered. Slowly she raised her hand and touched the glass of the monitor. She traced her fingertips over the screen, over the full-faced view

of her picture. For the first time in years Carley Mattea was pretty.

Through a mist of tears she said, "Please
make me look like that. Please give me back
my face."

She decided to begin her series of surgeries
over the upcoming spring break. "My teachers are accustomed to my spending time in
the hospital," she told her family. "Why
break the pattern? If everything goes okay, I
can have the second surgery over Christmas
and the final one next summer."

Dr. Chaffoo scheduled her CAT scan for
the end of February, but now that she knew
she could look normal, she was anxious to
begin the process, in spite of her dread of the
actual surgeries.

Carley was working in the backroom of
the bookstore on a Saturday afternoon with
Janelle. Together they were unboxing books
and chatting about Carley's upcoming trans-
formation. "I think it's super," Janelle told
her. "Too bad you had to wait so long."

"It's a little scary," Carley said. "And I
sure don't look forward to more hospital

time. Maybe they'll give me a discount. What do you think?"

Janelle giggled. "It's doubtful. Listen, I'll do your makeup when it's all over. Better yet, I'll treat you to a makeup artist."

"You will?"

"Absolutely. Only the best for my kid sister."

Carley dragged a box of books to a nearby shelf and, with her back to Janelle, began to stack the volumes on the shelf. "I'll be glad when this cast comes off too. Dr. Olson says another week—on Valentine's Day if you can believe it. You know, Janelle, this is the first time I've looked forward to Valentine's Day in years. Because once it's behind me, I can go for that CAT scan."

"Carley?"

She heard Kyle's voice from the doorway and froze. She heard Janelle pause before saying, "No. I'm Janelle, Carley's sister."

"But I thought—"

Carley's heart pounded and her knees quivered. Silently she prayed that Janelle would send him away. But even as she prayed, she could feel his gaze on her back.

Janelle said, "I know what you think. But it isn't true." Janelle took an audible breath. "That's Carley over there."

Carley gripped the side of the shelf to keep her knees from buckling. Then she heard Janelle leave the room and close the door quietly behind her.

Eighteen

Carley kept her back to Kyle and her gaze locked onto the covers of books inches from her nose. Her spine felt rigid. She heard him move across the room and stand directly behind her.

"Carley? Is this really you? Why did you introduce your sister to me and my friends and tell us it was you? I didn't even know you *had* a sister! What's going on? Tell me."

"Why did you come?" She ignored his deluge of questions. "You told me you would leave me alone after you came to the coffee shop."

"I wanted to see you," he said simply. "I figured if I came to the bookstore while you were working, your boyfriend wouldn't be a problem." He paused, then added, "But that guy in the coffee shop wasn't really your boyfriend, was he? He's your sister's boyfriend."

She saw no way around telling him the truth. "Yes. Jon is Janelle's boyfriend."

"Would you please turn around and talk to my face?"

She refused by shaking her head. "Would you please go away and leave me alone." It wasn't a request, but a demand.

"I won't go without talking to you face-to-face."

"There's nothing to say, Kyle."

"Why won't you look at me? I know it's you. I can smell your hair, all clean and sweet, like flowers. I'll never forget the way your hair smells. Please turn around."

She felt as if a knife was twisting in her heart. She had come to the end of the road. There was absolutely no way to avoid the inevitable any longer. No way to continue to hide the truth from him. She tasted the bitterness of defeat. Softly, with voice trembling, she asked, "Why do you think I don't want to look at you, Kyle?"

"I have no idea. But it's driving me crazy."
She felt his hand on her shoulder.

"Do you think my sister's pretty?"

"Sure, but— Is that what this is about?
You think you're not pretty?" He sounded
incredulous. "I don't care what you look
like."

"Really," she declared. Then slowly she
turned, until she was looking him in the
face. He was inches taller, but she raised her
head so that he could see her fully. Slowly
he removed his sunglasses. His skin looked
pink around his eye area, and moist with an
ointment of some kind. His lashes and eye-
brows, which must have been burned off in
his accident, were beginning to regrow in a
dark stubble. His eyes were a shocking shade
of intense blue.

As Kyle peered down at her, his expression was first one of shock, followed by disbelief and stunned silence. He took a step
backward. "What happened to you?"

She clenched her fists, digging her nails
into her palms, hoping that the physical
pain would replace the emotional pain and
keep her from crying in front of him. She'd

thought she'd prepared herself for such reactions, but she wasn't prepared. She remembered all the times he'd taken her hand and his face had lit up with a smile. But now he was seeing her in all her ugliness, all her deformity. "Cancer. When I was twelve. They cut it out, but left me looking like this."

"Cancer? Are you all right now?"

"I'm free of cancer," she said, but knew she'd never be "all right" in his presence again.

"But why didn't you tell me? Why didn't you say something while we were in the hospital?"

"I couldn't think of a good way to work it into the conversation."

His expression clouded, and anger formed lines around his mouth. "You should have told me."

"I liked having you think I was normal. It was a nice change for a boy to talk to me and treat me as if I were a real person. Instead of a freak."

"You aren't a freak," he said sharply.

"I'm hardly material for a modeling career, now, am I?"

"Why do you have to handle everything like it was a big joke? This isn't funny, Carley. You lied to me. Worse—you carried off a sneaky scheme to keep me from the truth. If I hadn't come here today, I'd have gone the rest of my life thinking you were somebody you weren't!"

She understood his anger, but she had no tolerance for it. "It was *my* face. My life. I didn't owe you anything. Stop criticizing me."

"You made out like we were friends. Like you cared about me."

"I did care. I—I just didn't think my physical appearance was any of your business."

He stepped closer and she felt the bookshelf against her back. "You didn't trust me," he snapped. "You figured that what you looked like would determine if I liked you or not. That wasn't fair!"

"I've seen the way guys look at me, Kyle," she fired back. "Can you believe that not one of them has ever looked me in the face and asked to be my friend? Or my *boy*-friend?"

He took her by the shoulders. "Well, I'm not like other guys."

"Right." She twisted out of his grasp. "If Steve and Jason had actually seen the real me that day in the hospital and said to you, 'Man, that girl is ugly,' what would you have done? Would you still have wanted to hang out with me? Would you still have asked me to your school's dance?"

He glared at her. "We'll never know, will we?"

She pulled herself up to her full height. "*I* know. Tell me, aren't you the tiniest little bit disappointed that I'm not the 'babe' you thought I was? Isn't there some small part of you that isn't totally shocked and disappointed? Remember, I saw your face just a while ago when you first looked at me. And I remember all the times you told me you thought I must be pretty." Now *she* was angry, and tired of being defensive about what she'd done. Kyle would never understand, *could* never understand what it had meant to her ego to have him believe she was attractive.

"All right, so long as we're finally being honest, yes, I'm disappointed. I'm sorry you're not what you wanted me to believe you were. I'm sorry you had cancer and that your face is messed up. I'm sorry I said things in the hospital to make you think your looks were important to me."

His words brought her no satisfaction. What had she expected him to say? "Then I guess we both got something out of this whole thing, didn't we? For a while you got to think I was pretty and I got to think some guy liked me. Too bad illusions can't be real life."

He glared at her without speaking, but she didn't care. As far as she was concerned, their discussion was ended. There was nothing left to say. Slowly Kyle slipped his sunglasses back onto his face. She wondered if the glare of the overhead lights had begun to hurt his eyes, started to ask, but thought better of it. No use letting him know how much she still cared about him. Better to make a clean break and put him out of her life once and for all.

He asked, "Do you know what I learned

when I was blind, Carley?" She shook her head, not trusting her voice. "I learned how to see. Corny, huh? I learned that vision can be a handicap because it allows us to make judgments based on what our eyes show us.

"Don't get me wrong, I'm very happy I have my vision back. I'm not sure I could have made it through a lifetime in the dark. But in some ways it would be good if everyone could spend some time without their vision. It teaches you what's important."

"Just like being disfigured teaches you," she countered. "But I'd rather have read the lesson in a book than experienced it."

He ignored her barb. "Do you know what blindness taught me about you?" He didn't wait for her to answer. "It taught me to see you from the inside out."

"Ugh—with all my blood and guts?" She'd tried to crack a joke.

He refused to be diverted. "I didn't come here today to embarrass you or to hurt your feelings."

"So why did you come?"

"All I wanted was to say thank you for helping me through my time in the hospital.

And to see your outside and how it fit with your inside."

"I'm sorry the match-up didn't work out," she said.

"You're right, it wasn't what I expected." He turned toward the door. "It wasn't what you led me to expect."

Tears stung her eyes, but she refused to let them escape. "I'm not sorry," she insisted. "Not one bit sorry that you once thought I was pretty. It was the first time in my life someone did."

"Well, I'm sorry," he said, pausing at the door. "I'm sorry you didn't trust me enough to tell me the truth."

She raised her chin, willing it to stop trembling. "When you tell Steve and Jason the truth, what will you say? How will you describe me? Don't answer. I know what you'll say. It's what everyone who ever sees me says. You'll tell them that my face is a wreck."

"Can a plastic surgeon fix your face?"

"Just this past week I met one who thinks he can. Funny, huh? If you and I had met two years from now, I'd be much more acceptable. Bad timing, Kyle."

He pulled open the door.

"By the way," she called. "I release you from your invitation to your school's Valentine dance. Believe me, it wouldn't be much fun for you with everyone staring at your date."

"It wouldn't be any fun being with a girl who didn't want to be there," he tossed back.

"This isn't my fault," she said stubbornly. "I gave you what you wanted: a pretty girl who kept your mind off your pain and problems in the hospital."

"You haven't even got a clue about what I want, Carley. And the sad part is that no amount of my telling you will make you know."

"Go away," she said. "I don't want your pity. And I don't need your charity."

He nodded curtly, stepped through the doorway into the busy bookstore, and was gone.

Nineteen

Carley moped for days after Kyle's visit. Secretly, deep in her heart, she hoped that he'd call. Not that she'd given him any reason to call her, but nevertheless she still held on to the hope that he might. But as the week passed and he didn't call, she abandoned hope.

She experienced a profound sense of nostalgia as the middle of February crept closer. She missed her days in the hospital when Kyle had "seen" her through the eyes of imagination. She thought about Reba and called her.

"How're you doing?" she asked.

"Wonderful!" Reba fairly bubbled into the

receiver. "I was thinking about you and wondering how you were doing. Did you and Kyle ever connect once you got home?"

Carley couldn't bear to go into the whole mess, so she simply said, "No. But I told you before I left the hospital nothing would come of us."

"Too bad. He was a nice guy and I thought he liked you a lot. I went to visit him after you went home, and all he did was talk about you."

The news twisted like a knife in Carley's heart. "But he'd never seen me," she reminded Reba. "Seeing me would have spoiled all his notions about me. Don't forget, Reba, love and beauty go together."

"Maybe not. I have a boyfriend and I'm no beauty."

"You do!" The news drew Carley up short. "Tell me about him."

"His name's Mike and he has cerebral palsy. We met at school, in our special ed. class. He's really super and he likes me, Carley. He's come over to my house and he's coming on Valentine's Day too. We're going to watch a video."

Carley felt a twinge of jealousy. Reba was in a wheelchair and she had a boyfriend. Jealousy quickly passed as she recalled what Reba's life was like. She said, "I think that's terrific," and meant it.

But after she hung up the phone, Carley felt more alone than ever. *Wait till I get my surgery,* she told herself. But it didn't help much. It might be two years before she looked more normal and by then high school would be over. And Kyle would go away to college. Their paths would never cross again and he would never get to know her without her scarred face.

What does it matter? she asked herself. She'd ruined any chance they might have had anyway. Still, she knew she would never forget him. Never. He was the first boy who'd ever treated her as if she were attractive. He was the first boy she'd ever loved.

Janelle was especially nice to Carley on Valentine's Day. She bought her a big box of chocolates in the shape of a heart. And her parents gave her a card with a gift certificate to her favorite department store. *But so what?* she thought. They were family and they always tried to make her feel better about the one holiday of the year she hated most.

Even Jon came through with a card for her. She told him thanks, but decided that he'd only done it to rack up brownie points with Janelle. Jon gave Janelle a dozen red roses, two cards, and a gold bracelet with a miniature gold heart dangling from it. It was pretty and Carley told Jon so when she sat with him and Janelle in the atrium during lunch break.

Students milled around the sunlit garden area waiting for the class bell to ring. "Want to come with us to the Mudpie after school?" Janelle asked.

"Mom's taking me to get this cast cut off," Carley reminded her. "Tomorrow I have to go to Rehab and really start working to get my leg back in shape." Carley was glad to turn down Janelle's offer. The last thing she wanted to be was a third wheel on Valentine's Day with Jon and Janelle.

Jon leaned back on his elbows. "No more Rollerblades?"

"Naw. I'm switching to bungee jumping."

Jon and Janelle laughed.

As they walked out of the entranceway door, they saw a crowd of students. "There's a plane buzzing our school," someone called.

"No way!" a boy shouted back.

"I'm not lying. It's dive-bombing us."

"Get on out here," Janelle called to Carley.

Carley sighed and hobbled along.

"I don't see anything," Jon said.

"He's coming around for another pass," a boy reported. "Just wait a minute."

"If this is your idea of a joke . . . ," someone else said.

"I'm telling you, the plane'll be back."

Carley heard the buzz of a small engine moments later. She gazed heavenward, and all at once saw the single-engine plane swooping down from the west.

"There it is! See, I told you," the boy shouted.

Fascinated, Carley watched along with the crowd of students as the plane dipped lower and lower.

"What's that guy doing?" Janelle asked.

"Beats me," Jon answered.

Carley continued to watch along with everyone else. Trailing behind the plane, she now saw, was a sign in big red letters.

"He's got a sign," Jon announced. "What's it say?"

"This must be some dumb advertising gimmick," another kid said in disgust.

As the sign unfurled behind the small plane, Carley couldn't believe her eyes. " 'Carley, Be Mine. K.W.' Who's Carley? Who's K.W.?" someone asked.

Carley's heart skipped a beat. She remembered what Kyle had said about his uncle and his own love of flying. Had he somehow persuaded his uncle to buzz the high school and fly the banner? Was Kyle in the plane with him? She read the banner again and laughed as she heard a girl say, "That's the most romantic valentine I've ever seen or heard about!"

On the other side of her she felt Janelle take her elbow. "You hate Valentine's Day? Kyle and you are through, huh? My, my, baby sister, remind me never to believe anything you tell me again!"

Carley stood speechless, watching the plane pull the long sign across the sky directly over the school.

"Are you saying this is the work of that guy, Kyle, from the hospital?" Jon asked, unable to disguise his disbelief.

"And very good work it is," Janelle cooed. She turned to Carley. "So what do you say now?"

Carley couldn't speak. A lump the size of a fist was clogging her throat. Kyle truly cared about her. Why else would he have gone to so much trouble and expense? Why else announce to the world he wanted Carley as his valentine?

"Actions speak louder than words," Janelle said in Carley's ear. "If I were you, I'd make one very important phone call as soon as you get home from the doctor's office."

Behind them Carley heard someone ask, "Who's Carley?"

She wanted to shout, "I'm Carley! Me! The girl with the messed-up face." But of course she didn't. The whole school would discover the identity of Carley. Janelle would see to that.

Elated and overwhelmed, Carley managed to answer Janelle, "I think I will make that call. I'd hate to leave the guy hanging."

Janelle groaned over Carley's bad joke, but Carley scarcely heard her. She looked up to see the plane cut a wide circle, dip its wing as if in greeting, and head off. The sign fluttered behind it in the wind, the large crimson letters stamped across the face of the sky, bright as the flare of a rocket.

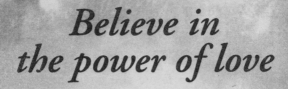